JASON AND DELILAH

Originality without compromise is rare in the world of Christian literature. When that quality is combined with genuine humour it can be irresistable.

This is quite simply one of the most entertaining and intriguing pieces of Christian writing that I have read for a very long time, and I wish I'd written it.

I forgive Simon however, and I strongly advise you to become acquainted with Delilah as soon as possible.

Adrian Plass

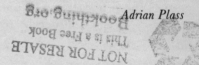

For Caroline
who patiently endured my flirtation
with Delilah. As Sebastian might say,
'Whoso findeth a wife findeth a good thing'
Proverbs 18:22.

Jason and Delilah

SIMON BAYNES

MINSTREL

EASTBOURNE

Front cover illustration by Vic Mitchell

British Library Cataloguing in Publication Data

Baynes, Simon
  Jason and Delilah.
  I. Title
  823'.914 [F]

  ISBN 1-85424-106-0

Printed in Great Britain for
Minstrel, an imprint of Monarch Publications Ltd
1 St Anne's Road, Eastbourne, E Sussex BN21 3UN by
Richard Clay Ltd, Bungay, Suffolk
Typeset by Nuprint Ltd, Harpenden, Herts AL5 4SE.

She can be as wise as we
    And wiser when she wishes;
She can knit with cunning wit,
    And dress the homely dishes.
She can flourish staff or pen,
    And deal a wound that lingers;
She can talk the talk of men,
    And touch with thrilling fingers.

Such a she who'll match with me?
    In flying or pursuing,
Subtle wiles are in her smiles
    To set the world a-wooing.
She is steadfast as a star,
    And yet the maddest maiden;
She can wage a gallant war,
    And give the peace of Eden.

George Meredith, *Marian* (1862), verses 1 and 3

Contents

Preface

These dialogues, like Dylan Thomas' poems, 'with all their crudities, doubts and confusions, are written for the love of man and in praise of God, and I'd be a damn fool if they weren't'. Such crudities, doubts and confusions as appear are because like Jason I am still a learner, and because I have not got a brain like Delilah and her peers. 'We feebly struggle, they in glory shine.' But the book is nevertheless a true essay in theology, for all its somewhat quirky style. The points made by Delilah and others can be paralleled in more serious books. Here are two examples.

Jason, attempting a little *l'esprit d'escalier* himself, tries to trap Harvey into admitting that Jesus is as much an historical character as Julius Caesar (page 86). F. F. Bruce writes:

> The historicity of Christ is as axiomatic for an unbiased historian as the historicity of Julius Caesar.

> *The New Testament Documents—Are They Reliable?* (Eerdmans, 1960, page 119)

Delilah dissuades Jason from buying a book on comparative religion, saying in effect, 'read the Bible and make up your own mind' (page 114). Tony Higton writes:

> In dealing with other faiths it is essential to know biblical teaching in order to assess their teaching.
>
> *Our God Reigns* (Hodder and Stoughton, 1988, page 138)

And Gavin D'Costa, an Indian Roman Catholic theologian, Secretary to the British Council of Churches Committee for Relations with People of Other Faiths, says much the same:

> For Christians a true evaluation and appreciation of non-Christian religions can arise only from a Christ-centred theology rather than a humanist-rationalist one.
>
> *Different Gospels*, ed. Andrew Walker (Hodder and Stoughton, 1988, page 224)

Research could find similar parallels for each point made. I say this, not to persuade the reader that the doctrine expressed is necessarily right, but to assure him that doctrines presented in the unfamiliar dress of comedy are nevertheless seriously conceived and deeply held. It is orthodox theology in unorthodox style; in Sir Philip Sidney's phrase, 'a medicine of cherries'.

The book is pure fiction, and any resemblance... etc. etc. You know the jargon. Besides the name of a parish secretary, only one short sentence is recollected history, the prayer Jason prays at 'SPACE'. Thirty-five years ago at a camp, a student whose name I still remember had recently come into a Christian experience, and prayed, 'Lord, thank you, thank you for all this. Amen.'

I am grateful to my son Dan for typing the manuscript, and to Colin and Lucy who helped. My warmest thanks are due to Tony Collins, Editorial Director of Monarch Publications, who first suggested the narrative form of the book and lent encouragement, enthusiasm and patience at every stage.

Quotations from the Bible are drawn from a variety of translations, as might naturally happen in the conversation of a group of friends, often quoting from memory and not necessarily word for word. I am grateful for the many good translations available, and acknowledge my debt to their publishers.

I

Billingsgate

You've never met Delilah Hewit? Ah. You've missed something. I pity you. No, I envy you. No, I don't mean that. Meeting D. H. is a kind of ambiguous experience. Ambivalous...valent. You reel away from the encounter as from a blow by Mike Tyson. And then come back for more. It's like a dream in which you find yourself embracing (I write from a male point of view) someone who is alternately Marilyn Monroe and Mary Whitehouse.

Delilah is living proof of how unfair God is. His hand must have slipped. He inadvertently gave an alpha double plus mind and an alpha double plus body to the same person. He did a much better job on Eve, who was seductive but stupid. That's a fair balance. But D. H. is a kind of genetic miracle. She's got far more genes than her fair share, and they stick out like the prickles on a hedgehog (speaking as a male hedgehog). Not fair.

The trouble with Delilah is that she's one of these ardent Christians, who know everything and believe everything, and then when she has proved that you're a backslider practically delivered to Satan to learn not to blaspheme, she suddenly turns all sweet and humble and loving and understanding, until you feel a worm and no man. I mean, I *know* the world wasn't made in six days. I don't know how I know it, I just know it. Then Delilah says 'How do you know? Were you there?' She does make the most absurdly naive remarks sometimes, but of course when she is naive you know that the superbrain is working over-time, and she is being deviously subtle. (I don't call that right, for a Christian. After all, Jesus said we must be harmless as doves, didn't he? And some-thing as something else, wasn't it? I forget the other bit. D. would no doubt give me chapter and verse, and quote it in the original Greek.) Then she will lecture me for twenty minutes on cosmology, demo-graphy and sedimentology, with extensive critiques of the day-age, gap and allegorical theories of Gen-esis, and ask me if I am not convinced by the argu-ments of Charles F. Pfeiffer. Have to admit I haven't actually read Charles F. Whoever, and find it dif-ficult to pronounce his name.

After all, I'm a perfectly good Christian myself, in a modest way. (Well, not perfectly good. You know what I mean.) A plain Christian. Nothing way out. I know I rank as beta minus in most areas. I've never actually gone in for *Mastermind* or the *Krypton Factor*. Delilah could probably do both, and win the Miss Bexley Heath title as well. It isn't actually her always being right that niggles me. Right is right, and if she is right—*if* she is right—well, that's all right with me. What niggles me is her always being right *and quick*. I am sure I could say the same sort of things as she does if I only had a little time to think about it. But she comes in with her upper cut while I am still hitching up my shorts. Metaphorically speaking.

'Avid?' she said to me the other day, looking as Cleopatra looked at Mark Antony when he dared to suggest that the Roman Empire was worth some consideration. 'Avid?', throwing my own word back at me as if it was a venomous dart and then poising her lips like a question mark, to which the only real answer was a smack. Or a smacking kiss. (I have never given Delilah a smacking kiss. Or any other kind. One day I mean to.) It rather takes you aback when you are expecting a lecture and all you get is two little syllables and a ranging shot from Delilah's eyes. All I had said was, 'I must admit I am not a very avid church-goer myself.' Which is true. I am a staunch supporter of the church. Staunch. But actually *going* to church is another matter. I am a very busy man. 'Delilah, I am a busy man,' I said, with patient British understatement. Besides, I do think too much church-going is a waste of time. And it can become fanatical. Over the top. So I repeat, I am not an avid church-goer. I go occasionally, to show my support. I don't know why D. H. picked on the word 'avid'. (Well, I do now. She's so fiendishly clever. Perhaps not fiendishly. Angelically?) Avid is not a word I use a great deal, but it seemed appropriate. I realised afterwards I had made a mistake.

'Avid?'

'Yes, avid. I mean, no, not avid. I am not an avid church-goer.'

'How avid is avid?'

'Delilah, you're splitting hairs.' (I couldn't help

noticing that her hair was looking especially lovely that morning.) But she persisted.

'Would you say that anyone who went to church twice a week was an avid church-goer?'

'Yes, I would. Definitely. Twice a week? Yes. Avid.'

'Right. Well, Jason, I am suggesting that you try being a non-avid church-goer for a trial period.'

'Non-avid?'

'Yes. Just once a week. OK?'

It wasn't OK, but she seemed to have won some kind of argument. I am sure there was a flaw in her logic somewhere (well there would be, wouldn't there? she's a woman), but I couldn't quite find it. Anyway, I did the honourable thing. (I try at least to be a gentleman.) I became a non-avid church-goer. For a trial period. I am glad I have that loophole. I think she slipped up there.

A peal of silvery laughter echoed down the High Street. That's how I would describe it. A peal. Well, it was something much less masculine and vulgar than a guffaw, less feminine and feeble than a titter. In fact, a laugh. A silvery laugh. Well, a laugh. That was it: just a laugh. And the laugh was Delilah Hewit's.

Now that I had started my career as a non-avid Christian, I was beginning to meet some of Delilah's weird friends, and I must say, compared with them she did seem remarkably balanced and normal. That laugh had a ring of blessed sanity about it; not bad considering she was being talked to by one of these friends who seemed drawn to her like a fly to flypaper. Sebastian. Seb is a chump, and spends half his time trying to score points off Delilah. He persistently calls her Miss He-wit, for instance, as if it rhymed with peewit. Delilah doesn't fall for that. She never minds if anyone pronounces her name wrong, or spells it wrong. Or calls her the wrong name. Or Mrs or Ms. She just smiles sweetly. Then Seb tries Miss She-wit. More appropriate, he thinks. Wit is certainly what Delilah has been given in full measure, pressed down and shaken together and running over. 'Just one of the minor gifts of the Holy Spirit,' she says modestly. (She seems to have all the major ones too. *Most* unfair.) 'Aha!' snorts Seb like the horse in Job when he smelleth the battle afar off. 'Not listed in 1 Corinthians, I'm afraid. Got you there, Del old gel!' Even this vulgar style of address fails to ruffle her.

'Word of wisdom?' suggested Delilah.

'Nope. Not the same thing at all! Wit in fact is an unbiblical concept. Doesn't occur once in Cruden's Concordance.'

'Like Billingsgate,' murmured Delilah, beginning to polish her nails.

Seb stopped dead, and as I was walking behind, I bumped into him.

'Billingsgate,' he gaped. 'Man, you can't be serious. Excuse the sexist language. Your brain gets more like God every day; it moves in a mysterious way. Billingsgate?'

'Yes, well, suppose I wanted a book on fish. Where would I go?' Delilah went on unperturbed.

'Book on fish.' Seb's mind clicked almost audibly as it digested this piece of data, and came up with a guess. 'A bookshop?' Then a wave of inspiration. 'A bookshop near Billingsgate?'

'Right. Maybe a bookshop near Billingsgate. Would you go to Billingsgate?'

'Er, no.'

'What would you find at Billingsgate?'

Seb looked as if he wondered what was coming next, the rack or the thumbscrew.

'Fish?' He ventured the syllable in a whisper.

'Fish. Exactly. Would you go to Billingsgate for a book on fish?'

'Unlikely.'

'Right. Let's assume there are no books on fish in Billingsgate Market. But there are fish. The word wit does not occur in the Bible. But wit does.'

She had got to the point at last, and even Seb seemed impressed. A discussion followed which featured camels, gnats, needles, brides and bridegrooms, planks and splinters, Jewish humour, Caesar, pennies, weeds and repartee, until one could almost hear the guffaws of the crowd of Hebrew villagers in the market place.

I was only a humble non-avid eavesdropper on this little dialogue, but it made quite an impression on me. My Bible had been forgotten on a top shelf for many years, but it struck me that the word of God was maybe not so dusty after all, and I decided then and there to give it another look. Then Delilah amazed us again. Somehow she touched a few buttons of that computer she keeps hidden behind the blonde curls and dredged up from the data bank of her memory a quotation from a sermon by Gerard Manley Hopkins, which stunned even Seb into an awed silence.

'No stories or parables are like Christ's, so bright, so pithy, so touching; no proverbs or sayings are such jewellery; they stand off from other men's thoughts like stars, like lilies in the sun.'

Stars, lilies, jewels, seemed to sparkle around us. I ended that day lost in wonder, love and praise. That sounds a bit over the top, I admit. Not really my style. But honestly, that's how I felt. The miracle was that I was not thinking about D. H. but about J. C. My ranking of him had gone up by forty per cent.

2

Weedkiller and the Chocolate Eclair

The next day was Friday. It was the end of March. On the 7.50 to town, yesterday's conversation kept buzzing in my head like a fly on a window, while I tried to concentrate on the F. T., the Budget and the Boat Race. I work in the City—which is good for my ego. I might be transferred any time to Basingstoke or Wolverhampton, but meanwhile I am in this insurance office in Lime Street. I find the phrase useful at parties. 'In the City,' I say airily, and they step back a couple of paces, awed by an image of plush carpets, commissionaires with top hats and turtle-soup dinners. I don't disillusion them. If they want to imagine me having lunch with Tiny Rowland once a month and hobnobbing with the Directors of Lloyds, it doesn't worry me. In reality life is rather less exciting.

Delilah's absurd arguments nagged at me. I could hardly remember the points she was trying to get across, her methods were so devious. But somehow I was left with a shattered image, and the possibility of something more wonderful, something fresh and new and of dynamic power, coming together to take its place. A jaded image of a long-haired, long-faced guru with sad eyes and a voice something like a cross between John Gielgud and Billy Graham, surrounded by a crowd of eager peasants, beautifully mouthing Tudor prose, replaced by—just what? No clear picture as yet, but only the idea of wit always intruding. A witty man. Argument. Repartee. Stories. Jokes. A man who laughed.

I had to admit, I mused, pouring out of London Bridge station with the crowds, I had never before imagined him laughing. A laughing Jew. And there was another thing. I had never imagined him as a Jew before. Much too blue-eyed. But if he was a Jew, and laughed, that made him—well, it made him real, for a start. So that was it. He had never been real before. Now he seemed as real as Delilah, and you can't get more real than that. Delilah laughed, and yet she took this man with total seriousness. What would he look like, I wondered, if I met him in the crowds jostling over London Bridge? Like any other Jew? And there were plenty of them.

I made an effort to concentrate on the day's work ahead, until a sign marked Billingsgate hit me in the eye (not literally, I am glad to say), and the whole extraordinary dialogue came flooding back. God seemed to be getting at me. What would happen next?

All day I was immersed in *any other country in the respect of which the Commission of the European Economic Community is satisfied that arrangements have been made to meet the requirements of Article 7 of the EEC Directive on insurance of civil liability (No.72/166/CEE)*, and other

long sentences, and returned on the 5.25, vaguely
hoping as I did every day that the 5.25 would have a
very minor derailment leaving me with a very minor
broken ankle and £40,000 in compensation to be
collected. God, if he was as wonderful as they made
out, might at least arrange that. He had done
nothing much so far, I felt, to reward my moral
suburban existence. I could do with a few more Acts
of God working in my favour.

Instead, on this particular day, the 5.25 behaved
with depressing atheism, not even offering me a seat,
and arriving fourteen minutes late. It must have
been working for the Enemy, who also organised a
heavy shower on arrival, so that I got back to my
unlovely digs sodden and mutinous.

I could not face an evening in, but was fairly
broke, so went in search of food, trying to calculate
whether McDonald's or the Kowloon Golden
Dragon would work out cheaper, when I noticed the
church coffee shop. This was a little place at one end
of the High Street called The Meeting Place, which
doubled as a bookshop. I had never been in, as the
window always seemed to offer titles like *Dynamic
Marriage: Putting the Glow Back into your Partnership,
You Too Can Have the Gift of Tongues* or *The Times of the
End: Fifty-Two Eschatological Questions for Busy Executives*. It was, however, open, and promised 'Inexpen-
sive Snacks' and 'Light Meals' besides the
theological goodies, so I slipped into this temple of
avid Christianity as anonymously as possible, edging
past the stacks of audio cassettes featuring The Last
Days Bethesda Choir, Randy McClune, South Car-
olina's best-loved rock gospel singer, and the Word
of Wisdom Ministry in Song. The food looked quite

normal, and I was gratefully sidling into a darkish corner with my jacket potato, soup and salad when a ray of sunshine from another table beamed on me, and there was Delilah, with Sebastian and Mandy Ayres, a friend who lived with her.

'Hello, great to see you,' I said, and meant it. 'Filthy weather.' I meant that too.

'Lucky to have any weather at all,' was Delilah's characteristic reply. 'Come and join us.'

She was looking as neat and well-groomed as if she was just off to the studio to make a commercial for holidays in Tunisia. That was the sort of thing she probably did; I hadn't yet discovered. I joined them.

But as I sat down I almost wished I hadn't. On the table among the quiche and spaghetti was an open Bible. So we were in for some more do-it-yourself R. E. I salted my potato as meekly as possible, and for quite a time managed to remain uninvolved.

'Gardening?' Mandy was saying. 'What's that got to do with it?'

'We were discussing the injustice of the world,' explained Sebastian, for my benefit. 'No proper incentives for good behaviour, no real deterrents to being a crook. Mafia chiefs and big-time drug-pushers with their millions living it up in Hawaii without a worry in the world, and we poor honest suckers doing everything right, and toiling away on starvation wages without recognition.' He gloomily filled his mouth with chips. 'The whole thing doesn't seem to be organised on sound capitalist lines at all.'

'But why gardening?' repeated Mandy. She was a librarian, and liked things neatly classified. Delilah seemed to attract bookish friends.

'The art of gardening,' put in Sebastian irrelevantly 'is to train the slugs to eat the bindweed.'

'I was thinking of weedkiller,' said D. H. 'Ever used it?'

'Can't remember. May have. At my parents' place. Why?'

'Well, the way it works,' mused Delilah. 'I suppose there are different types, but one type works by overstimulation. I remember seeing dandelions in the lawn that had been treated, and they were shooting up much higher than the grass.'

We began to get the point.

'They out-grow their strength. For a few days they look as if they are grooming themselves for the Chelsea Flower Show. Then, wham! They've had it.'

'Sounds like the British economy,' I murmured. 'Overheating.'

'Exactly.'

'Trouble is,' said Sebastian 'those crooks in the Bahamas seem to last more than a few days. Perhaps a little more application of the weedkiller is needed there. Verdone in their champagne. Hm. Nice idea.'

But his dreams of becoming a professional assassin employed by God were not to materialise.

'We leave that to God,' said Delilah.

'But he doesn't do it,' complained Mandy.

'He does it in his own way and in his own time,' said Delilah seriously. 'That's what we find hard to take. But look at the big political tycoons. Hitler. Mussolini. Idi Amin. President Marcos. Ceausescu. Noriega. There is usually a point of reckoning.'

'But this weedkiller stuff,' put in Mandy. 'It's not very biblical is it?'

'Let's see,' said Delilah and thumbed the Bible till she came up with Psalm 37.

> 'I once knew a wicked man who was a tyrant;
> he towered over everyone like a cedar of Lebanon;
> but later I passed by, and he wasn't there;
> I looked for him, but couldn't find him.
> Notice the good man, observe the righteous man;
> a peaceful man has descendants,
> but sinners are completely destroyed,
> and their descendants are wiped out.'

'And come to think of it,' added Mandy, 'Jesus told a story about weeds, in among the wheat. Remember? Let both grow together till harvest.'

A thoughtful pause ended. Time for reflection. Some chewing of the cud.

'Hm.'

'Hm.'

'Hm.'

'Pudding?' said Delilah brightly, getting up. 'Coffee?' We moved to the counter, I wondering if I could afford an ice cream. I was next to D. H. in the queue. A nice place to be. I found myself saying quietly, 'I wish I had your faith.'

There were actually other attributes of Delilah I wished I had too, but that was the word that came out.

She stood quite still in front of the counter, not looking at me, as if thinking deeply. At first I thought she hadn't heard. Then she spoke.

'Wouldn't it be wonderful to have that chocolate eclair. I *wish* I had that chocolate eclair!'

She reached out and took it.

Really, Delilah can be quite greedy sometimes. I chose coffee only.

3

My Backhand Volley

'How about tennis?'

This was a new line, jerking me out of a reverie in which Idi Amin swelled to the proportions of a cedar of Lebanon, turned into a giant dandelion, and then toppled to the ground. I was also in a stew of righteous indignation about the eclair. How could Delilah think of eating chocolate eclairs? How could she afford them? Besides, it was Lent, and weren't Christians supposed to give up things like chocolate eclairs in Lent? Worst of all, how could she eat chocolate eclairs and still remain that tantalising 34–24–34? (I haven't actually measured Delilah, though I would be happy to oblige if she wanted someone to do it any time; but by the look of her, she must be pretty close to those dimensions.) There was another instance of God's unfairness. No justice at all. In that mood I was almost ready to put people who ate chocolate eclairs in Lent, and near the end of the month, when other people couldn't afford them, in the same league as Idi Amin. D. certainly could be described as flourishing like a green bay tree (or cedar of Lebanon, as her crass modern translation put it).

But tennis? What was she going to make of that? Her thought processes really intrigued me.

'Tennis?'

How was she going to relate backhand volleys down the line to faith, justice, cedar trees, weedkiller....

'Do you play, Jason?'

Do I play! Just wait till she sees my backhand volleys down the line. My curling second serve. My angled smash. My—

'What about a game tomorrow?'

It gradually dawned on me that she was talking about tennis. The game. Not about the righteous man and his descendants. Did I play? I certainly did. And a game of tennis was just the thing to sort out the men from the boys, the people who kept themselves in training from those who ate chocolate eclairs. Not that I wanted to show her up in any way. But I was not averse to a little mixed doubles now and then. I said yes. Tennis with Delilah—what could be nicer?—as long as she left her Bible in the changing room.

'Sorry, I don't play,' said Mandy.

'I'll ask Jessica,' said Delilah.

'Ten o'clock?'

This struck me as a bit too keen. I am a very busy man, I work flat out all the week and often take work home in the evenings. Saturday is my one chance of a lie-in. And I told them.

'Idle so-and-so,' said Sebastian rudely. 'Why don't we make it eight? With half an hour's jogging beforehand to warm up.'

I would have thrown a roll at him, only I couldn't afford one. Instead I merely remarked with dignity, 'Watch it, Seb. This is supposed to be a Christian Coffee Shop, you know. Don't let's lower the tone.'

Eventually they agreed to eleven o'clock. A much better hour for tennis. We City men have some responsibility as guardians of civilisation. Besides, it would give more time for the rain to clear up.

So it was at five to eleven next morning that I rolled up in my eight-year-old Metro, hoping that the others would have arrived first and paid for the court. They had. Moreover I was surprised to hear the call 'Five–two' as I strode onto Court 16. There was Delilah, looking cool and steady as usual, lighting up one end, and Sebastian lumbering about at the other. They must have been playing for half an hour already. I was not entirely surprised to realise that it was five–two in Delilah's favour. Sebastian has some powerful strokes, but they are usually out by about three yards. And Delilah—well, I could see at a glance that she was a natural. With those legs that God had given her, she just had to be a tennis player. Perhaps—good heavens! the thought struck me for the first time—perhaps she was a pro. A coach. Perhaps that's what she did. She was certainly a sporty type. Well, not a sporty *type*. Just sporty. Delilah isn't an anything type.

They stopped their singles—'Too bad, I was just coming back from behind,' put in Seb—and we gathered at the side of the court. Jessica arrived at the same time, and as we were saying hello I noticed among the sweaters Delilah's Bible. She seemed to carry it everywhere, like a flag. It niggled me; one of her little weaknesses. Like chocolate eclairs. I am glad she had some. It wasn't a proper Bible, anyway. Not what I call a proper Bible. It was sort of bright and happy-looking. Almost paperback. Not in very good taste.

'What's my share? I'd like to contribute,' I said airily, jingling the coins in my pocket, mostly coppers. I am nothing if not generous.

'That's all right, this is on me,' Delilah said to my relief. 'Next time perhaps. Now how do we play?' I was to partner Jessica, who was a teacher—I hoped a P.E. teacher—at Brooklands Comprehensive.

'P.E.?' I queried, eyeing her somewhat beefy form.

'Sorry, no. R.E.,' she smiled sweetly.

Good Lord, another nut, I groaned. What I actually said was, 'How very interesting.' Manners at least I do maintain. I wondered if I was being set up for the next phase of my Christian education. We tossed for ends.

'Do you know the one about the two bulls?' said Sebastian, who was addicted to corny jokes. 'They were put in the same field. One said, "Let's toss for ends!" ' Polite laughter rippled across the court as we started to knock up, I trying to keep my eye on the ball and not on Delilah's legs.

We found ourselves well-balanced. Jessica played in a solid, methodical way, getting everything back, never attempting a smash, apparently content for every rally to continue for twenty shots. Sebastian was on good form. Every first serve that went in, which was at least one in ten, was unreturnable. My game is subtle. I play with my head. My finesse is usually too much for Sebastian. I have him floundering on the baseline while I drop my shot just over the net.

Delilah was superb. If she was not a pro, she

played like one, with total dedication, total concentration on every shot, and without the least show of emotion. Her shots were not always in, and her serve was not strong, but what I admired was her anticipation. With perfect footwork and balance she was always in position, and then backlift, stroke and follow-through were executed with the style and timing of a master.

Jesus was forgotten for two hours. Delilah's Bible lay unopened on the bench. Del and Seb won the first two sets, the second going to a tie-break which I lost in a moment of inattention. D. jumped and stretched to reach a high ball near the baseline, and I was so lost in admiration of her perfect form that I did not recover quickly enough to reach her lob, which sailed over my head.

The third set was equally hard-fought, and when Sebastian won it for us 6−4 with a sizzling drive that hit the back net without touching the ground, we were all ready for a break. Especially me, after my very heavy week in the City.

A long cool drink and then lunch together at the tennis club. I hoped we could get through without a theological discussion, but in the end it was I who started it. Fool. I just couldn't get used to this Bible-carrying habit, and it seemed extraordinary that Delilah had to make such a thing of it. There was something crude about it. Washing your clean linen in public. I wondered if it worked like a lucky charm for Delilah; a talisman; a mascot. When we had discussed the game, I couldn't help butting in.

'Well, I must try bringing my Bible next time. And I'll make sure it's a bigger one than yours, Delilah! Then perhaps God will be on our side.'

It was worth a cheap crack to hear the effect it produced. An uninhibited peal of laughter, which turned many heads in our direction. The hills were alive with the sound of music. Would have been, if there had been any hills in SE2. I hardly needed an answer. It was clear the idea was ridiculous to her. She merely said, 'I lost last week.'

I couldn't help pursuing it. 'But why do you carry a Bible everywhere?'

'I love it,' she smiled disarmingly.

There was no answer to that. But at the same time the idea of anyone actually loving that ponderous collection of ancient texts was new, disturbing and hard to believe.

'Don't you?'

I couldn't focus immediately on D.'s challenge.

'Er, well, no I can't say I find it riveting. I mean, I respect it, of course. It's the foundation of our system. It has made us what we are. Absolutely. The Bible and Shakespeare. Magnificent prose....' I was getting into a mudbath of pompous blather, I realised too late, and Delilah was the last person to try that out on.

'Ever read it?'

I might have known that was coming. Touché.

'Well I read the best parts. I discriminate. One must look at it with a certain critical detachment.' I began to regain some self-respect. Jessica, I felt sure, would be on my side.

'Some of it is frankly not very edifying. But one sees a certain refining process at work, and at its best it produces some great works of art. Passages of great significance and beauty. A thing of beauty is a joy for ever,' I added gratuitously.

'Such as?'

Why did I ever get into this, I thought.

'Such as...well...the Sermon on the Mount, for example.' I was on safe ground there.

'Wow!' Delilah sat back in her chair and sucked her drink through a straw. 'Strong stuff! Not for beginners, I'd say. You really believe in hell fire?'

'Hell fire? No, I most certainly do not! A barbarous idea. Primitive. A hangover from ancient Jewish mythology. No, I said the Sermon on the Mount. Consider the lilies of the field. Solomon in all his glory. The high peak of Jesus' teaching. Really sublime. That's what I can accept.' I only then noticed that Sebastian was chortling away and seemed to be enjoying a private joke with Delilah. He had opened her Bible, and now read:

' "If your right eye causes you to sin, take it out and throw it away! It is much better for you to lose a part of your body than to have your whole body thrown into hell." Matthew five verse twenty-nine. The Sermon on the Mount.'

These Bible buffs, they really are rather tiresome. I mean, you can prove anything from the Bible. At the same time, though I couldn't believe in hell fire, I couldn't help being a little chastened by that particular saying of Jesus, because during the conversation my right eye had been preoccupied with the contours of Delilah's bust underneath her thin nylon blouse. My left eye wasn't entirely blameless either.

The discussion ambled on, ranging from lilies of the field to the kingdom of God and his righteousness, and for the most part I lay low and listened. I tried to take a polite interest in Jessica and her work. I hoped at first I might have found an ally in her.

After all, R. E. teachers can't survive in the class-room without a certain amount of healthy scepti-cism. Forlorn hope. I soon discovered to my horror that I had met a sample of that threatened species, the R. E. teacher who actually believes the Bible. As I said before, Delilah seemed to collect the weirdest types.

I escaped as soon as I could after lunch. Our parting conversation went like this.

D. H. (making my day): 'Well, thanks for the game, Jason. I really enjoyed it. Your backhand volleys down the line are a treat.'

J. E. (modestly): 'Thanks. I'm afraid my service needs a bit of working on.'

D. H. 'See you tomorrow then.'

I hadn't realised we were going to play again tomorrow.

J. E. 'Oh, er, yes, fine. I'll look forward to that.' Which I did, except for my moneyless state.

S. G. 'Your service tomorrow, J. Ten o'clock, right?'

J. E. 'A bit early, isn't it? Couldn't we make it…'

S. G. 'Sorry. There's no service later.'

I suddenly realised what kind of service he was talking about, and remembered my promise.

'Oh hell!' I blurted out involuntarily. 'I mean, yes, fine, of course, I'll be there. Ten o'clock. Right.' I tried to calculate how little I could decently put in the collection.

Delilah rose like Solomon in all his glory. 'You don't believe in hell,' she said.

Game and set to Miss Hewit.

4

I Go to the Comedy of Errors

Going to church next morning recalled the first conversation I had with Delilah, a week or two before.

'I honestly think too much going to church is bad for the character,' I had said. 'After all, most people who go to church are hypocrites.' I was not alone in thinking this. I have heard lots of people say it. I realised too late this seemed a bit of an insult to her, the last thing I wanted to suggest; but this particular blonde hypocrite smiled sweetly and said, 'Isn't that rather a superior attitude?'

I couldn't understand that. 'Why superior? It's true, isn't it?'

'But you are making yourself better than people who go to church.'

'No, I'm not at all. It's just the opposite!' (Was this girl a little thick? Dumbness and blondness had been known to go together before. This was before I got to know her.) 'It's the people who go to church who think they are better than others.'

She wasn't convinced. 'But you say they are mostly hypocrites.'

'That's right. Not all, I agree, but most of them.'

'And is being a hypocrite a good thing?'

How naive can you get? I tried to be patient. 'No, of course not.'

'And you're not a hypocrite yourself?'

'No. Of course I'm not perfect, but at least I'm not a hypocrite.'

Then she came in with what she considered her punchline. 'And people who go to church are. So you're making yourself out to be better than them. Right?'

I was still trying to work this out two weeks later. It was like one of those geometrical tricks consisting of a lot of cubes piled up, and the stairs go up one way, and then you realise they can't. Really, women shouldn't go in for logical arguments. They are no good at it. They only confuse us. And I am not a hypocrite!

So here I was, preparing to meet all these hypocrites. I hadn't been to St Paul's since Christmas Eve. I met Sebastian at the corner and we went along the High Street together. He was carrying a Bible, the same sort as Delilah's. I hoped we wouldn't meet Harvey, crawling out to buy his cigarettes at the corner shop. Harvey is a friend who also works in the City. An estate agent. We often meet on the train. Mercifully, a quarter to ten is a bit too early for him.

Sebastian was his usual unsquashable self. The Sunday lethargy which descends on most of my friends did not touch him.

'The dear old C. of E.,' he prattled. 'Shakespeare

wrote a play called *The Comedy of Errors*. Some people think that's what C. of E. stands for.'

Jokes on a Sunday morning are not my style. We went in to the lobby. Gentle but lively music greeted us, and an expectant hum of conversation. I was given a couple of glossy books that looked a bit like holiday brochures.

'What's this?' I asked Sebastian.

'Hymns,' he said.

'Not the hymns I know,' I returned. 'A & M, isn't that the usual thing?'

'Ancient and More Ancient,' he replied. 'You wouldn't choose your furniture like that, would you? Nothing later than 1950?'

We went in. I was amazed to see the church three-quarters full. Jessica was waving from half-way up. She was keeping places for us. 'You have to come early if you want a back seat,' she grinned.

I looked round. People were talking, laughing, embracing everywhere. Children swarmed. There was, I might have known, a mass of electrical equipment up at the front, where a group of three were playing. An overhead projector. Two microphones. There were even television screens dotted around. The complete electronic church. Yes, a comedy of errors, certainly.

'Where there is no television, the people perish,' muttered Sebastian. 'Proverbs 29:18. Revised Version.' The bustle went on. I couldn't get used to this overfamiliarity in church. People actually hugging and kissing each other. Quite wrong.

The church filled up. We were invited to sing. I sang. Actually, I have a good voice, and a good ear, and I wasn't afraid to let others know. In fact, I really enjoyed it. The singing was rich, but not strained. I forgot myself, and was quite uplifted. Only when we stopped I realised that I had never heard the hymn before.

We sat down, and I suddenly thought of Delilah. Where was she? We were keeping a place for her—I was keeping a place for her, right by me. Unlike her to be late. I looked round but couldn't see her anywhere. The gap she left was almost tangible. I kept a lookout for her, so that I could beckon her to her place when she appeared. At least it was the sort of church where I didn't feel embarrassed at looking round. There was plenty of quiet movement, people coming in late, greeting friends, children happily wandering.

I began to quite enjoy the relaxed atmosphere. Notices were being given out by two people alternately. I couldn't help thinking of Morecambe and Wise. Little and Large. The Two Ronnies. The notices seemed to go on a long time, interspersed with news of individuals and items for prayer. Now and then they called others up to the microphone to share some personal news.

The friendly atmosphere was making an impression. Maybe there was something to be said for a little friendliness. A warm but discreet gesture of fellowship. A dignified embrace. Nothing too hearty. A civilised greeting. Yes, perhaps it was acceptable.

Strange that Delilah still wasn't with us.

Laurel and Hardy were coming to the end of their act. I heard 'finally'.

'...plans for space are going ahead well,' said Laurel. 'Six people have handed in their booking forms already this morning, which brings the total to eighty-four.' There was a hum of applause. Hardy chipped in, 'In case there are any newcomers here today, we had better explain what SPACE is: St Paul's Away weekend for Challenge and Enjoyment.' I had wondered.

'That's right,' resumed Laurel. 'May 12th to the 14th. And there are still a few places available. Let's go for the hundred!'

Another buzz of agreement.

'You too?' said someone in my ear. It was Jessica.

'I think not,' I murmured politely. 'I'm a very busy man.' What I really meant was, not on your life. Not my scene, these hearty weekends away where you have to enjoy the fellowship. I mean, I am all for challenge. I respond to it. But I draw the line at enjoyment.

We sang again. A Bible reading came next. Most people seemed to get out their own Bibles and follow the reading. The Delilah-shaped blank remained at my side.

The passage was Joshua chapter 1. I made a mental note of it, so that I could tackle Delilah afterwards. This Old Testament stuff about the Jews marching in to other people's territory and bagging it—nothing had changed! Blatant land-grabbing. Aggressive imperialism. Hitler and Poland. Russia and Afghanistan. Really quite unacceptable. And the sheep piously bleating at the end:

'This is the word of the Lord.'

'Thanks be to God!'

There was a New Testament reading, more military stuff about the armour of God, and wrestling with principalities and powers, and the sermon, most of which went rather over my head. I have enough to cope with every day, wrestling with liabilities and claims. (Sebastian agreed afterwards that it was a bit airy-fairy for his taste too. 'This is an age of church history,' he quipped, 'where the buildings get more and more concrete, and everything else gets more and more abstract.')

The service ended with a crescendo of praise which no doubt set everybody up for a week of battling with the principalities and powers. Again I enjoyed the singing, though most of the hymns were new to me, and some of the words went against the grain. But I got a pagan satisfaction from being part of what was in fact a mass choir—like singing The Messiah from scratch. I even had a fleeting sense of worship—though who or what I was worshipping remained dim. A golden contralto at my side would have completed the pleasure, but wasn't there.

We poured out, most people hanging about to talk and laugh, buzzing round the well-stocked bookstall with its glossy paperbacks, records and cassettes, an extension of The Meeting Place ('Half our congregation are bookworms,' said Sebastian, 'and the other half are tapeworms!'), inspecting the extensive notice boards, or overflowing into the hall for coffee—and there at last was Delilah. She had been sitting right at the back on the other side. Avoiding me? She looked as if she was just off to have lunch with Princess Diana in the royal box at Ascot. Well, not actually wearing a hat. But otherwise...I wondered where she got her clothes. Or did she make them? Perhaps she was a dress designer? Nothing more likely. I could just see her in something like *Howard's Way*, selling modes to top people for 500 guineas each. Did they still talk about guineas?

'I love Joshua, don't you?'

A typical Delilah remark. Provocative. Love! Any of that precious commodity I happened to have wasn't going to be wasted on this sort of thirteenth-century-BC Yasser Arafat.

'Isn't that a bit naive?' I suggested, as we drifted through for coffee.

'Of course! I love naiveté, don't you?' You just can't win with Delilah.

'I don't see how anyone can love naiveté.'

'It's what we're all aiming for. Simplicity. *O sancta simplicitas*!'

'If it's the simplicity that simply marches in and grabs other people's territory, I think we can do without it.' I thought that was a telling point and rather well put.

'Yes, I agree. I don't like that bit either.' I was taken aback. Delilah had conceded a point. I pressed my advantage as we sat down round a table.

'Most of the Old Testament is unacceptable. It's all this aggressive military stuff—' ('Ruth?' she murmured, stirring her coffee. Really, she ought not to take sugar in coffee. Unhealthy.)

'—this aggressive stuff about blood and violence and utterly destroying this that and the other.'

'But it's *real*,' she said.

I paused for a moment, and took a biscuit. Jessica now joined the battle, obviously psyched up by the sermon and the singing to wrestle against the powers of darkness in the shape of poor innocent me.

'Surprising how the kids love it in school,' she said. 'Delilah's right, it's the realism that appeals. That's why it has survived all these centuries. If you want a lurid description of a prostitute—'

'I don't, thank you,' I protested. Really, these liberated women...

'—you can go to T. S. Eliot or Graham Greene, or you can go to Proverbs chapter 7. It's devastating.'

' "Death, like cancer or crime or copulation, stands out real!" ' put in Delilah. She has this knack of obscure quotations.

'If I was a teacher I wouldn't give too much of that to the kids at school,' I said. I thought R. E. teachers were supposed to be guardians of the nation's morals.

'But seriously,' Delilah went on, 'what I like about the Bible is that it is so down to earth. It's God coming into the everyday world of farming and marriage and child-bearing and the market place and petty crime. It's human. It isn't whitewashed. It isn't bowdlerised. It's earthy. Life as it is.'

'Absolutely.' This was Sebastian. 'I rather like that bit in Leviticus 21 about "a blind man or a lame, or he that hath a flat nose, or anything superfluous, or a man that is brokenfooted, or crookbackt, or a dwarf, or that hath a blemish in his eye, or be scurvy or scabbed, or hath his stones broken". Earthy.'

He must have learned this off by heart from the Authorised Version simply to try and score cheap points off Delilah. Sebastian is supposed to be on the side of the angels, but he will do anything for a laugh. Delilah withered him with a we-are-not-amused glance. 'Nut,' she said crisply.

'God coming into the everyday,' I mused. 'Fine, if he does. But I don't quite see it happening. I wish I had your faith.' I had the feeling of having said this before recently.

'Much better stick to your own,' said Delilah decisively.

'But I haven't got any. I've lost it.'

'Like a credit card?' she came back. 'Excuse me, I've got to meet someone.' She stood up.

'Credit card?' I held her coat.

'Yes, if you lose one, it doesn't mean you can never get credit again. Either your card is recovered, or you're issued with a new one. It's not the end.'

I followed her to the door, trying to digest this. 'But I don't believe in God any more.'

Delilah turned at the door, and her glorious smile was like God coming into the everyday. She uttered one word, with the ecstasy of Rutherford when he split the atom.

'Hurray!'

I was stunned.

'Excuse me,' she said. 'I must fly.' She flew.

I returned to my digs trying to fathom what on earth she meant. When I got in I took down my Bible and read Proverbs chapter 7.

5

The Empty Seat

March turned into April, bringing gales, newborn lambs, and a pay packet. The squally weather put a stop to tennis for the time being. Bottoms Up won the Grand National, I lost a fiver, Oxford won the Boat Race for a change, and Sebastian came up with some predictable foolery for April 1st. The end of the financial year brought extra pressure of work; I missed church and did not see Delilah for a week or two. Then, solvent again, I rang her up to invite her to a concert.

Mandy her flatmate answered.

'Delilah's away. She's on holiday.'

This was a blow. How could people go away before April 5th? Irresponsible. Here was I slaving myself to the bone, and looking forward to a well-earned night out, and Delilah goes off on holiday.

'Seems a funny time to go on holiday.'

'Yes, well, Delilah never does the obvious. That's her. You know?'

I knew. I suppose anyway that in dress design or

modelling or TV commercials or whatever it was she did the financial year was not important.

'When is she back?'

'She'll be back for Easter.'

'Ah. What does she do, actually?'

'She works in London. Some sort of business office. You'll have to ask her, I'm a bit vague. Something in the City.'

The City! All sorts of ideas leapt at me. What on earth was she? PA to the Governor of the Bank of England? Interior decorator at the Mansion House? Intriguing.

'See you next Sunday, Jason?'

I came down to earth.

'Er, next Sunday? Oh yes, of course. At St Paul's. Yes, I'll be there. Right. See you then. Bye.'

'Bye.'

I hung up, still absorbed in the vision of Delilah walking down Threadneedle Street, Delilah greeting guests at the Guildhall, Delilah sweeping into the Stock Exchange, turning all heads.... But a voice remained with me, not Delilah's. Mandy's. A kind and patient one, a little plaintive, detached and half-amused. It slowly dawned on me that I had been rather rude.

I rang back straight away.

'I say, Mandy, you must think me very rude. Fact is, I'm rather overworked at the moment. Under pressure. But what I meant to say was, would *you* like to come to this concert? Wednesday week. At the Festival Hall. I've got two tickets. It's Bach. The St Matthew Passion.'

'Oh. Thanks. Sounds a nice idea. Let's see, Wednesday week. Yes, I'd like to. Thanks.'

'Great. I'll see you Sunday, then, and give you all the details. Bye.'

That evening I got down my Bible and did some homework. I wanted to have some tough questions ready for Mandy and the others on Sunday. Having read Proverbs chapter 7, I now went back to the beginning and read the book right through at a sitting. A strange book to start on, perhaps, but not a bad one. I found it somewhat repetitive, but entertaining.

There was no doubt it underlined what Delilah had said about wit. Here was the same Jewish verbal slapstick bursting through the gold edges and black cover of my Authorised Version: 'A continual dropping in a very rainy day, and a contentious woman, are alike.'

It was the voice of Groucho Marx from three thousand years ago. I made a note of one or two bons mots to surprise Sebastian with, like: 'As the door turneth upon his hinges, so doth the slothful upon his bed.'

Not forgetting to learn the reference, 'Proverbs 26:14'.

The last chapter amused me, with its cosy picture of the ideal Jewish momma—not entirely unlike my image of a possible future Mrs Enderby, with some allowances made for the passing of three millennia—until it began to merge with another female figure who worked in the City and said surprising things: 'She openeth her mouth with wisdom; and in her tongue is the law of kindness.' Her parting smile, and that baffling 'Hurray!' still haunted me. There didn't seem much wisdom in that; but no doubt there was some hidden meaning, which she would explain one day.

I was now somewhat bitten with the idea that this strange volume could actually be read, and was not just something one did in R. E. at school (the last time I opened mine). I thought I had better go back to the Sermon on the Mount and really see what it said, so I decided to work through Matthew's Gospel systematically, making a note of all the problematic passages as I went along. I almost got grounded in the first chapter; I had forgotten all those 'begats'. A question from the start: did Jewish carpenters really trace their descent from Abraham? It was a bit like Sebastian claiming that his family tree went back to Edward III. But I plodded on, pencil in hand, spurred by the thought that this was meat and drink to Delilah. I imagined her on the Costa del Sol stretched out on the beach in a bikini and dark glasses, a long cool drink on one side and her open Bible on the other. Here, the English spring had set in with its usual severity, and April was weeping its girlish tears outside my window, gleefully hammering home the essential injustice of life.

At the end of the week I went along to the public library, determined not to be beaten by a few begats. I thought I would get hold of a commentary on Matthew's Gospel, and see how it explained all the hard bits. Then what was left, what it couldn't explain, would be really strong stuff to challenge Delilah with. I would ask Mandy to recommend a book.

An unknown woman was at the counter.

'Excuse me, is Mandy Ayres here?'

'No, I'm afraid not. She came in this morning, but she had to leave early. To go and see the doctor.'

'Is she ill?'

'Well, you know she has been under the doctor for some time.'

(I didn't.)

'She gets these dizzy spells now and then.'

'I see. Er, could you tell me where the religious section is? Bible commentaries and so on?'

She told me. All I could find was a weighty tome that covered Genesis to Malachi and Mark to Revelation as well. I lugged it back to my digs, reflecting that the theologians were in on the act of modern sales technique; you go to Sainsbury's for a lemon and have to buy a packet of a dozen. God getting at me again? Saying, 'Look, this is my word, take it or leave it. This is the treatment. If you're a Christian you read the lot. Right?'

I wasn't too convinced.

I dutifully went to church that Sunday, where there was a visiting preacher who sounded like an American acting Othello, trying to reach an audience that must have been sitting somewhere near the Dartford Tunnel. And they forgot to turn the microphones off. I christened him the prophet Elijah. He must have been a bit stupid, as he started off, 'I am not coming to you with any man-made theories or philosophies. I am coming to you with the simple old-fashioned gospel. I am not preaching any -isms or -ologies. My method is straight-forward evangelism based on sound theology.' At first I thought it was meant to be a joke, but I had to suppress my amusement as no one else was laughing. I was so taken with this that I missed most of the sermon in the effort to remember it and relate it to Delilah. One other gem I picked up near the climax. 'We need to be on fire for God!' Elijah enthused, in a voice that made the windows rattle. 'We need to burn for God! Henry Martyn said "Let me burn out for God!" ' (I cast a professional eye round the building at the mention of fire, imagining the whole thing going up in smoke, and assessing the claim. Seven figures certainly.) 'I was talking to an African brother in Christ last month and he said, "We need to be drunk with God!" That's right, isn't it? The church today needs God-intoxicated people, right? And that's a very sobering thought. Ay-men, brothers and sisters?' A reverent 'Ay-men' came back from the congregation, but it was not quite God-intoxicated enough to satisfy Elijah, so he turned up the decibels and repeated 'Ay-men?' The response apparently passed the test, so he turned to prayer with, 'Let us all pray,' which was difficult, as the prayer seemed to be more Elijah-intoxicated than anything else. I was interested that he did not pray to Jesus, but to J-e-e-e-esus, and that he used the word Lord as a comma.

I met Mandy and Sebastian afterwards.

'Enjoy the service, Jason?' asked Mandy brightly.

'Oh yes. Like the dentist.'

'As bad as that?'

'No, not bad at all. I mean, I enjoy going to the dentist. I like reading the magazines.'

'Point taken. So it wasn't entirely to your taste?'

'Well, as I say, I really do enjoy parts of it. I mean, the singing. You've really got something good there. It's not Bach, but it's good of its kind. But Elijah...'

'Elijah?'

'The prophet Elijah. That's what I called him. What's his name?'

'Ah yes, our fiery friend.' This was Sebastian. '*Ein Gottbetrunkener Mensch.* Not your style? I rather agree. Even I found the verbal pyrotechnics a little too much. The trouble with evangelical preaching today is that it's a hangover. The fag-end of a tradition. It's the fallout from an explosion that happened four hundred years ago.'

'Maybe,' I said. 'But why do they have to have these transatlantic celebrities preaching? I mean, this is an Anglican church. At least I thought it was.'

'Quite right,' said Sebastian solemnly. He was in his most ebullient mood. 'Let's stick to the Book of Common Prayer. The Queen, God bless her. I believe in God the Father Almighty, maker of Great Britain and Northern Ireland. No, the Church of England is doomed. Let's join the Baptists for a quiet life.'

'You can joke about it,' said Mandy, who had obviously been moved by the sermon, 'but there is such a thing as spiritual renewal. The Holy Spirit is at work in all denominations. God is moving in the church with a quiet revolution.'

'Quiet? Not quite the word I would have chosen,' went on the irrepressible Sebastian. 'I forgot to bring my earmuffs this morning. But I'm all for revolution. Let's go for it. Up the Red Flag. There's a lot to be said for a Red Flag,' he went on, 'as long as it's got a white square in each corner. God for Harry, England and St George. Long live the C. of E.' And he burst into song.

'Yet in spite of all temptations

To belong to other denominations
He remains an Anglican,
He rema-a-a-a-ains an Anglican.

Apologies to Gilbert.'

I felt rather sorry for Mandy, who was not in the mood for Sebastian's tomfoolery.

'How are you feeling, anyway?' I managed to turn the conversation to her at last. 'What did the doctor say?'

'I'm fine. I'm normally all right. It's just some condition that hits me now and then, and I pass out occasionally. They haven't got to the bottom of it yet. I've got to go in for more tests after Easter.'

'That's a worry. Anyway, I'm glad you're feeling better. And I'm looking forward to Wednesday.'

'Oh yes. Thanks a lot. That'll be great. I really love Bach.'

We made arrangements to meet, and then parted.

The Delilah-less days dragged on. I spent some time with Matthew's Gospel, the commentary and a notebook. The commentary was fairly good at saying at some length what commonsense might deduce, and skating over the questions I really wanted to ask, so I abandoned it and stuck to the text only. The one thing the commentary did provide—and this amazed me—was pages of evidence for the reliability of the ancient manuscripts. I began to get quite absorbed, and to wish I could read it in Greek. Instead I went to The Meeting Place, taking care not to meet anyone there, and bought a modern translation of the New Testament. I avoided the one with the garish cover like Delilah's.

Wednesday came, but no Mandy appeared in the foyer of the Festival Hall. I waited. Is anything more frustrating? I particularly dislike being late for plays and concerts, but I waited till five minutes past the hour, then left Mandy's ticket with a message at the box office, and had the humiliating experience of pushing past people's knees to reach J23 and being thought a Philistine.

I was not prepared for what happened to me that night. I was fairly conversant with Bach, and I had been to plenty of Masses and Te Deums and Requiems before. I normally enjoyed the music while being no more emotionally involved than when listening to Tosca or Lohengrin. Tonight was different. Previously if I became absorbed in Bach it was to be time-warped into the eighteenth century. Now, I was in the first. The music was the familiar background of a journey that took me back to the simply told events which seemed the beginning of history. The words of the Gospel I had been trying to reinterpret now came to me like a personal message. The language came to life, the scene lived. I was there.

I cannot describe the experience except by saying that I had an acute sense of being alone and not alone. Was it by design that Mandy was not there? I knew no one among these thousands, and did not need to. I was on a different planet from my shirty neighbours, who probably suspected that I was capable of pulling out a packet of crisps during a chorale. The music, the words and I were all that existed. At the same time I felt very much not alone. The empty seat beside me became a symbol. An unseen counsellor seemed to sit there, tracing the score with a finger, illuminating the words, guiding me through the landscape, the upper room, the garden, the way of sorrow. I sat very still, as if expecting someone to tap me on the shoulder. I did not clap at the end, and the clapping of the thousands was like a welcome crowd applauding something I had done, where I had done nothing. I stood mechanically and waited while J24 to 30 shuffled out, turning round and staring at my seat as if even that had a message for me.

J23.

My initial, my age.

So what?

The next morning I rang the library. Mandy had collapsed at the station last night and had been taken into hospital.

6

Easter Day

The Festival Hall glowed in my memory. Whatever had happened was decisive. Unanswered questions teemed in my brain, but one thing was clear: the incontrovertible reality of God. Where it left me I had no idea, but I knew I would never be quite the same again. Bach may have been God's agent, but nothing could efface that wonderful aloneness, the sense of a personal encounter. It was as real when I drew the curtains on to a dull sky at seven the next morning as it had been the previous night. The commonplace suburban scene, the cars, the commuters, were the ambience of a new reality. I had known moments of excitement at concerts before, but they ended with the music. Now Bach was very distant, but the presence I had felt seemed to belong equally to the world of lamp-posts and dustbins. Delilah's phrase came back to me: God coming into the everyday.

We were extra busy in the office the last two days before the Easter break, and I did not get to visit

Mandy till Saturday. Meanwhile Jessica had rung up to invite me to join her and a few friends for a picnic on Easter Monday. They were going out on the Downs somewhere. I gladly accepted. It might be a good chance to discuss Matthew. The odd thing was that I wanted equally to share my new vision of the gospel and what it had come to mean to me, and also to tackle the problems, the absurdities, the inconsistencies which made it so hard to swallow as a whole. Anyway, it would be good to get out in the country. I needed a break. And perhaps Delilah would be there.

'Delilah will be coming, and a few others,' said Jessica on the phone. 'She's back tomorrow, I think. Anyway, I'll see you on Sunday.'

'Yes, fine. See you. Goodbye, and thanks.'

Jessica, I mused, putting the phone down; the athletic Scripture teacher. Sebastian, yuppie and all-round comedian. Mandy, delicate, book-lover. Delilah... There was another funny thing. They mattered, yet they did not matter. None of them had been there last night, none of them had helped me, none was a midwife assisting at a new birth. It was God and me together, God and me alone. And yet without them nothing might have happened. Without them, I would not have been galvanised into reading Matthew's Gospel, and without that reading the concert would have been no more than any concert, nothing but the memory and a programme in a bottom drawer. 'Life' was the simple word which summed it up, all that I had discovered, all that mattered. 'Life, life, eternal life!' — the long-forgotten phrase came back from *Pilgrim's Progress*. No other prayer, no other explanation seemed necessary.

And here I was, feeling rather stupid with a bunch of grapes, asking for Ward 7. I wasn't very good at this hospital business. I found Mandy polishing her glasses, fully dressed and chatting to another patient in the day room. She was calm and cheerful.

'Hi, Jason. How sweet of you to come. I'm terribly sorry about the concert. I hope it didn't ruin it for you.' I stared, as the memory came flooding back; the music, the words, the empty seat.

'No, it didn't spoil it for me. I missed you, but...well, I'll tell you about it one day. But how are you? What do they say?'

'I'm fine. Fighting fit. Ready for a ten-mile hike. I'm going home tomorrow.' I felt embarrassed about the grapes. Not the right thing.

'Grapes!' said Mandy. 'How marvellous. Everyone brings me flowers, till I feel like a corpse. I'm ravenous. Let's gorge them now! Mrs Farrar, have some grapes.' I appreciated her tact.

I was in the act of trying to remove pips gracefully and drop them in the paperbag when a presence announced itself in the day room; a whiff of scent, a flurry of skirt, a flash of colour—and Delilah was here. I felt a surge of irrational joy. She was tanned from her holiday.

She embraced Mandy, friesias in one hand. 'Flowers, how marvellous!' said Mandy. 'Here's Jason stuffing me with grapes and I'm going home tomorrow.' We all laughed. I was glad I had come.

We left together. I was conscious of male heads turning in our direction. I told Delilah about the concert, and tried to describe the indescribable. She seemed to know something had happened. In the car park she stopped, looked at me very straight, and said quietly, without smiling, 'Hurray.'

'You said that before.'

'Yes. So I was right.'

'You were right. But I don't see how...'

'Come to lunch tomorrow, and we'll talk about it.'

'Great. Thanks, I'd love to. By the way, what is wrong with Mandy? Do you know? The nurses wouldn't tell me.'

'Leukaemia.'

She got into her car and drove off.

I drove home in confusion. I could not understand how joy, shame, anger, fear and total happiness could so obstinately co-exist. God had given me a box of chocolates and a slap in the face at the same time. But God was God.

Easter Day was an explosion of sunshine, a fanfare of daffodils, a cabaret of wonderful talk, singing, music, laughter, jokes, plans, food, fun, and the *lachrymae rerum* of life. The resurrection of Delilah. The reality of Jesus. The tangible givenness of the word. The frail presence of Mandy. Clouds passing over the sun like reminders, like blessings, like punctuation marks in the April sentence. Life, life, eternal life. I had never been so happy before. Correction. I had never been happy before.

I met Sebastian and Jessica at the church door at half past nine. We went in, keeping seats for the others, and the church was soon full to overflowing. St Paul's was a pastoral symphony in green, yellow and white. Sunshine flickered over everything. The music was well chosen. There was no visiting preacher; all was harmony. Delilah came in rather late, having put things in the oven for lunch, glowing with health, looking like the very spirit of Easter. The singing was tremendous. There was a sizable orchestra to lead it, not just the group of three. There were precious times of silence. Perhaps for the first time ever I knew what worship meant. Perhaps for the first time I experienced holy communion; the peace that passes understanding; songs of everlasting joy. Only half way through the closing act of praise did I notice that Delilah, ever unpredictable, had gone.

On my way to Delilah and Mandy's flat, I bumped into Harvey coming out of the corner shop with his fags and Sunday paper. Harvey is a bit of a wimp really. He dresses, speaks and acts as if he was pretending to be an old Etonian. He is definitely not an old Etonian, but he has a kind of flashy brilliance that conceals a certain hollowness within, and most girls think him good-looking. It was fairly obvious that I had been to church, and the funny thing was that I did not feel in the least defensive about it.

'See you there next Sunday?'

My first essay in evangelism was not a success.

'Not on your life!' he replied cheerfully. 'See you on the 7.50 on Tuesday. Or for lunch. It's your turn to buy me a drink.' And we went our ways.

We gathered for lunch at the flat, and there was Mandy looking cheerful but pale, especially against Delilah's suntan. Sebastian was his usual self. He breezed into the kitchen.

'Is this the face that launched a thousand quips?' he clowned.

He hovered about the kitchen, lounging against the sink when Delilah wanted to get to it, picking things up she put down, chattering non-stop and generally getting in the way. At last lunch was ready and we sat down.

Delilah prayed a simple prayer. 'Thank you, Lord, for our being together today. And thank you for Jesus. Amen.'

It was just what I wanted to say for myself. I suddenly realised the great thing that God had given me over the last few weeks: friends.

Conversation sparkled over the lamb and mint sauce. I had lots to talk to Delilah about. Her holiday, for a start.

'Where did you go? Madeira? Tenerife?' Maybe somewhere even more exotic. These people with top jobs in the City...

'Lincolnshire.'

'Lincolnshire!' This girl had an inexhaustible fund of surprises. 'But how did you get the suntan?'

'Not much sun, I admit. Mostly wind! It has the same effect. We were out all day, every day. Tramping the fens. Birdwatching. It was superb. You want to try it sometime.'

I could almost see Sebastian's mind working away, trying to make a joke out of this, but he didn't quite make it in time. I pictured Delilah knee-deep in water with binoculars face to face with a red-necked phalarope. Or did I mean red-legged?

'I'd love to. Let me know when you're going next.' I really hoped she would.

'We could start tomorrow, if you like. I'll bring my bird book.'

'Oh yes, the picnic. Great. Why not?'

'As long as you don't expect to see gannets on the North Downs!'

'OK. Fine. By the way, Delilah, why did you leave church early?'

'I went to pick up Mandy from hospital. They said she could come out at eleven o'clock. She had to wait and see the doctor first.'

'I see. But surely she could have waited another half an hour? It was such a wonderful service. I really felt that. Wasn't it hard to leave before the end?'

'I'm glad you enjoyed the service, Jason!' she smiled. 'But church isn't everything. God doesn't live in church. If you really love God, the only thing that matters is people.'

I paused to think this out, a new potato poised on my fork. The extraordinary remark seemed to ring a bell inside me. Was it something from the *Oxford Dictionary of Quotations*? A bon mot of some famous saint? Or a Delilah original? Someone ought to collect her sayings, like Boswell and Johnson. God doesn't live in church—how uncannily she echoed my experience! God had met me in the Festival Hall, not first in St Paul's.

A superb pavlova followed, smothered in cream. After lunch Mandy went upstairs to rest. She was determined to come with us on the picnic the next day. The doctor had said she could live normally, but must take care not to get tired. We took our coffee out onto the little patch of garden behind the flat, and basked in the sun. Delilah handed round bits of a giant Easter egg she had been given by some admirer.

Jessica and Sebastian were discussing the sermon. I pulled my chair nearer to Delilah, who was sitting on a beanbag. Her bronzed legs sprawled on the grass.

'Why "hurray"?' I asked her quietly.

She smiled. 'You said you didn't believe in God. That could mean two things: he doesn't exist, or he apparently exists, but he has no meaning for me personally. You meant the second, right?'

'I suppose I did.'

'And if it was the second, I knew you were on the way. Not far from the kingdom. You were at least *talking* about God, even though you didn't believe in him. The *word* God existed for you. That was quite a big step forward.'

'Yes, I suppose so. But how did you know?'

She looked long and hard at a daisy held in her fingers. 'I just knew. Perhaps it's what Paul calls "the gift of knowledge". I suppose you would say feminine intuition.'

I digested this. It rang true, though I had a niggling feeling that Paul would not have entirely approved of a girl having the gift of knowledge. I mean, he was a bit anti-feminist, wasn't he? But then he had never met Delilah.

Question followed question in my mind. Mandy, resting upstairs, overshadowed everything. Kindness and cruelty mingled strangely in my thoughts. Why should such happiness have to do battle with these doubts, so soon; a real approach to love be tinged with this bitterness?

'Why is God so cruel?' I was so absorbed in my own train of thought that it was a mild shock to find Delilah answering, 'Parents are pretty cruel, too, sometimes, aren't they?' I had not realised I had spoken aloud.

'Parents? What have they got to do with it?'

'Children get hurt, don't they?'

'You mean child abuse?'

'No. Accidents.'

'I don't follow. If it's an accident, then it isn't the parents' cruelty, is it?'

'I wonder.' Delilah was thoughtfully filling up our coffee cups. 'A kid of four is riding a tricycle up and down the drive. Gets excited. Goes too fast. Gets out of control. Out in the road. Doesn't see the lorry coming. Then, wham, it's all over. Tragedy.'

She paused to drink. I couldn't see what was coming next.

'Well?' She was obviously waiting for a feed, and some more of her strange illogical logic was on the way. 'So what?'

'How can parents be so cruel?'

I pondered. She had made some kind of a point, though I couldn't quite see how it applied. I had to ask for enlightenment. Patiently she explained.

'We live in a dangerous world, right? We're walking on ice. Accidents happen every day. Disease is all around us—germs, viruses...agreed?'

'Agreed.'

'So we have to take risks, and parents have to let children take risks. You can't keep them in cotton wool. You have to give them freedom, within limits.'

'Yes, I see that.'

'But they still love their children just as much!'

'Of course.'

'So why does God get blamed when people are hurt? He is like a parent. He still loves us. But he gives us freedom, which includes freedom to get hurt.'

I chewed this over. It couldn't be the ultimate answer, of course. Her argument must be flawed. I would have to take time to think it through. But for the moment it made God less of a problem. It made him a little more human. No, I don't mean that. Or do I? The suffering Mandy seemed to be wrapped in parental love, and that was greatly comforting. But oh, why did God have to be so paradoxical?

'The goodness and severity of God,' murmured Sebastian, who had heard the last part of our conversation. 'Romans 11:22.' It was one of his more apt quotations, though hardly solving anything. It described but did not explain. I almost envied Harvey with his bland atheism. Wasn't that simpler, after all? I would like to see Delilah tackle Harvey! He wouldn't be so easily convinced.

'It baffles me,' I said. 'There's no real answer to the problem of suffering.'

'Whatever else suffering is,' cut in Delilah, 'it isn't a *problem*.'

'Not a problem?'

'Of course not. You make it sound like chess, or a crossword, or algebra.'

'I agree,' said Jessica. 'Christians don't have problems. They have an enemy.'

More lessons in theology. Could I really trust these rather way-out believers? Were they sound?

'But you make it sound as if you have all the answers,' I retorted. 'That can't be right. It's oversimple.'

'We don't have all the answers,' Jessica came back at me, 'but we have The Answer. And you have too, now, Jason.'

Had I? Is that what I had? It didn't seem like it at the moment.

'You're beginning to sound like some of these fundamentalists,' I complained.

'I am a fundamentalist.' This was Delilah again.

'That's right.' Sebastian ensured that we did not get too serious. 'Delilah should be on the coins, instead of the Queen, with F. D. after her name. Defender of the Faith. "Mighty through God to the pulling down of strongholds!" Two Corinthians, somewhere.' His microchip memory failed him for once.

'Try chapter ten.' Delilah pushed her Bible across the lawn to him.

'But you're not really a fundamentalist?' I said uneasily.

'Funny how people hate that word,' mused Delilah. 'I regard it as rather an honour, if I am seen to be sticking to the fundamentals. People are so wary of being labelled fundamentalist. It's like saying, "I have decided on the whole, with certain mental reservations, to accept the V. C." Personally I admire fundamentalists. Like William Blake.

> If the sun and moon should doubt
> They'd immediately go out.

All the great saints are fundamentalists. Francis of Assisi. Julian of Norwich. Mother Teresa...'

'The Ayatollah Khomenei,' put in Sebastian, straight-faced, echoing her tone.

'That's another matter, which we'll have to discuss one day,' said Delilah unperturbed. 'But really, to get back to the point, this "problem of suffering" business bores me stiff.'

She lay back on the beanbag and shut her eyes. I stared. The word 'bored' was so unexpected and so inappropriate that I couldn't make her out. And there was a sharp tone in her voice that I hadn't heard before. Angels would have feared to tread near Delilah at that moment, I realised afterwards; but in I rushed.

'*Bored*?' I emphasised. 'How can you say that, when one of your best friends is chronically sick?'

She answered with steely quietness, her eyes still closed.

'I am bored with talk about problems. Problems have solutions. Solve your problem if you can. So what? How does that help Mandy? It's totally academic. Help Mandy if you like. Pray for her. Spend time with her. But don't discuss her.'

I was chastened. 'I'm sorry, but...' (Why can we never learn to say sorry, full stop? But I had to try and justify myself. Like a fool. Couldn't I see what would follow?) 'I'm sorry, but actually we weren't discussing Mandy. We were discussing God.'

Delilah sat up, her eyes blazing. 'That's ten times worse. Hate God if you like. Curse him. The psalmists do. Taunt him for being asleep. Grumble at him. Pester him. Give him no rest...'

('Isaiah 62,' murmured Sebastian mechanically. How insensitive can you get? And how could he possibly remember such an obscure reference anyway? I sometimes think he bluffs.)

'...but don't discuss him.'

Nobody moved. The sun blackened and dazzled, the afternoon stillness shouted, the grass turned all colours. I had never seen Delilah angry before. It was like the wrath of God. Somehow we got back to normal, and went in to do the washing up. When we left it was with a sense of deepened understanding and acceptance, and a determination to pray for Mandy night and day. As a focus of fellowship the kitchen sink is sometimes better than a church.

As we were clearing up I saw with a shock the label on Delilah's Easter egg. It was from Harvey.

7

The Lord is My Butcher

On Monday the five of us drove out to the Downs in two cars. The fine weather held. I had a strange sense of doom-laden happiness. Clouds are naturally dangerous things to walk on. Today, anyway, I would enjoy to the full.

We did a gentle walk along the Downs, taking care not to tire Mandy. She was determined to come with us. Delilah seemed to know the place well. She was soon pointing out woodlarks and meadow pipits that no one else had noticed, but by the time she had handed over her binoculars, and I had got them focused, they seemed to have gone back to their woods and meadows. A kestrel I did see. Even I could tell that it was not just a rook. The hovering was unmistakable.

' "The achieve of, the mastery of the thing!" ' quoted Mandy.

' "My heart in hiding stirred for a bird",' came back Delilah. They shared this love of Hopkins. 'The Windhover. He said it was the best thing he ever wrote. And it's about Christ.'

I couldn't quite see the connection, but it was a fine sight anyway. It was good to see them both so happy. Another quotation followed, as we wandered on.

' "How good is man's life, the mere living, how fit to employ
All the heart and the mind and the senses for ever in joy." '

This time I stared. It was Mandy who had spoken. Could she mean it? How long was her 'for ever'?

'Do we have to bring the library with us?' complained Sebastian. 'We philistines would rather enjoy the country neat, thank you, without the literary stuff.' His own serious reading was confined to the Bible. 'Sexist language, anyway. Doesn't it worry you?'

'That's nonsense,' said Delilah serenely. 'What the militant feminists have never admitted is the simple fact that man is two different words. Homo and vir. It's a plain defect of the English language.'

Mandy joined in. 'Exactly. There are thousands of words the same. You buy a pound of tomatoes, and you hand over a pound to pay for them. They are two distinct words. There's no danger of confusing them in your mind.'

'Hmm, you've got a point there,' agreed Sebastian. 'Anyway, less of the Eng Lit, if you don't mind, Mandy. Just because you went to a posh university.... It upsets the balance of nature. The bar-tailed godwits don't like it.'

Jessica exploded in giggles. 'How ignorant can you get? Godwits are sea birds.'

'Just the point I'm making. They don't like literary ladies. They keep away.'

'Quiet, everybody.' Delilah cut short the banter. She had her binoculars trained on a bush on the edge of a copse. We stopped obediently.

'A long-tailed tit. Just on the left side of that gorse bush. Low down. Black and white. Do you see it? I think there's a pair. They should be nesting.'

We gazed hopefully at this ornithological wonder. I vaguely saw something move.

'A pair of tits. How interesting.' Really, Sebastian is impossible. I glared at him. He opened his mouth, thought better of it, and shut it again.

'The smallest of the tit family,' went on Delilah unperturbed, handing her binoculars to Mandy. 'They're fascinating. Someone took one of their nests to pieces and counted two thousand feathers. Very domesticated. Birds without eggs actually help the ones with families.'

'Unlike those beastly robins,' mused Jessica. 'Remember Mr Pocock?' She smiled at the recollection.

'What happened?' We wanted to know the story.

Delilah sat down with the binoculars, elbows on knees, to get a better view of these specimens of *Parus acredula caudata*, while we wandered on. Jessica related the saga of Mr Pocock to the rest of us.

'Mr Pocock is one of these Greenpeace nuts. You know, he believes all we need is to get back to living in harmony with nature. He says Christian values are repressive.'

Mandy joined in. 'That's right. He actually said, "Animals and birds have so much to teach us. We need to get back to nature." Crazy! And Del just said, "Like Robins, for instance?" He fell right into the trap.'

Jessica went on, 'Yes, poor old Mr P. "Of course," he said, "like all birds. But why robins especially?" Delilah gave him her usual dazzling smile, and said, "Rather horrid little birds, don't you think?" '

She chortled at the recollection. I couldn't quite understand the point about robins. 'Why robins? What's wrong with robins?' I wanted to know.

'That's what Mr Pocock said,' Jessica explained. ' "Robins? They are beautiful. I sometimes think they are nature's little messengers to man." Or some twaddle like that!'

Mandy: 'And then Delilah simply said, "They fight." Mr P. couldn't understand it. "Fight? Robins?" '

Jessica: 'So Delilah explained. "They really are one of our most aggressive wild birds, actually. They will even attack their own species, and occasionally fight to the kill." Poor old Pocock hummed and ha'ed, and said, "Well I suppose sometimes they have to fight to survive..." So of course Delilah said, "They certainly do. So 'back to nature' is rather naive, isn't it, as a recipe for a peaceful society? 'Nature red in tooth and claw', you know." And Mr P. mumbled something like, "Well, yes, Kipling would see it like that, wouldn't he? I mean, he was a warmonger, wasn't he?" And Delilah came in with the coup de grace. "So perhaps Christian values are worth considering after all? Tennyson, actually!" '

'Very clever,' said Sebastian. ' "A word spoken in due season, how good is it!" Proverbs 15:23. Poor old Pocock. He'd better brush up his knowledge of wild-life.' He smiled as the word recalled a joke. He collected jokes as Mandy and Delilah collected quotations.

'Wildlife. Remember that good one about the local Wildlife Society? There they are in the village hall making whoopee with balloons and streamers and blaring music. On the door is this notice saying "LITTLE SODBURY WILDLIFE SOCIETY ANNUAL DISCO". Outside there are a few birds dozing on the trees and a couple of squirrels asleep. And one rabbit is saying to another, "No wonder they're called a wild life society!" '

The discomforter of Mr Pocock was meanwhile intent on scanning the heath for signs of whinchats and wheatears. We stopped for lunch, settling Mandy as comfortably as possible against a tree.

'It's funny how exclusive we are in the types of people we accept,' began Delilah, who had half heard the Mr Pocock story.

'I admit I wasn't very kind to poor simple Mr Pocock.' 'We know your idea of a good conversation,' said Mandy, munching. 'Like Dr Johnson. "You tossed and gored several persons." '

'But people are so ridiculous,' put in Sebastian. 'I collect them. I've got a little list. They'd none of them be missed. Preachers, for a start, who dissect the Gospels, and treat them like racing cars. You know, Mark I, Mark II, Mark III...'

'People in church who put their hands in the air when it's totally inappropriate.' This was Jessica's contribution.

'I've heard that in the Pentecostal churches,' said Sebastian, 'somebody says at the end of the meeting, "Hands down who would like coffee." '

'And people who see evil spirits under every bush,'

went on the down-to-earth Jessica. 'You know, some of them say "So sorry to hear you've got this toothache. I believe it is a spirit of oppression. We must pray for you to be delivered." And everyone has a ministry of this or that. It's like Whitehall.'

'Ah yes, ministry. Blessed word.' Sebastian looked grave. 'Actually, I have a ministry myself. A ministry of deliverance.'

'Do you think you could deliver us from these ants?' I put in facetiously.

'Sorry, I can't run to that. Not my department. Union rules, you know. No, last weekend I delivered 150 letters around the parish for Graham.' (Graham was the vicar of St Paul's. Everyone seemed to use his Christian name.) 'My ministry of deliverance. Most important.'

Even Mandy laughed.

'And who's on your little list, Mandy?' Sebastian turned to her.

'People who tell corny jokes, of course,' said Mandy sweetly. ' "All funny fellows, comic men, and clowns of private life." No, not really. You help to keep us sane.'

Delilah stood up.

'Well, if everybody's finished, who's coming for another walk?' she said. 'I want to explore that wood.'

'I'll stay with Mandy,' said Sebastian drowsily. Was he being noble? Or lazy? He was lying flat on his back in the sun with his eyes closed.

'Have a good bird-hunt,' he said. 'If anyone spots the gold-crested double-breasted He-wit, let me know. Haunts tennis-courts and churches. Gregarious, but can be aggressive. Song something like the nightingale, only flat. Eggs large, brown, chocolate-coloured.'

Delilah laid a thistle gently on his recumbent form.

'Ass. Look after Mandy. We'll be back in an hour or so. Bye.'

The three of us went off in the direction of the wood. I immediately broached the subject of Harvey. Was he really a friend of Delilah? Yes, apparently, they had known each other for some time. I don't know why, but this really niggled me. Harvey was my friend—well, a kind of friend. We had been at school together. Why should I resent his knowing D. H.? Yet I did. I was even more hurt when I heard that Harvey had been one of the group who had been to the Fens with her. Don't say Harvey was one of those birdspotters? Yes, it seemed, he was an expert. Much better than Delilah herself. This again was something I didn't know. Then why hadn't she invited him today? She had, but he had to go and see his family.

Delilah and Harvey. What could be more incongruous? It almost spoilt my day thinking about it. It was worse when I actually pictured them together. Physically, they would make a superb pair. Harvey was tall and well-built. I had to admit he was handsome. Not so incongruous perhaps. Thoughts gnawed at me. Was Delilah...?

But they were totally incompatible. Harvey was an outright atheist. I pursued this line with her.

'I'm really surprised at you and Harvey being friends. I mean, I didn't think you had much in common. I suppose it's the ornithology?'

She evaded a direct answer, and chose to be enigmatic.

'Ornithology and humanity, let's say.'

'Meaning?'

'I like him, for goodness' sake!'

Was she really taken in by Harvey? He was a rather superficial person. Perhaps she hadn't yet discovered his brilliant qualities; as brilliant as tinsel.

'But I'm afraid he doesn't share your faith.'

'And I don't share his taste for garlic.'

Worse and worse. She actually knew all about his likes and dislikes. She was being defensive, but I pressed on.

'I thought perhaps you found the company of Christian friends more congenial?' After all, I had only ever seen her in the company of other Christians.

'Like a knife in the drawer with other knives? Hardly what knives were made for.'

I could see that her razor-sharp mind was always on the attack, and that underneath the laid-back style she was ever doing battle for the church militant. I found it hard to reconcile myself to this aggressive form of Christianity. But again she changed tack.

'What are Christians in our society? Five per cent? Maybe less. If you limit your friendships to Christians it could be a bit stultifying!' And then, simply, 'I like Harvey.'

This correspondence will now cease. Editor. I took the hint, and changed the subject.

'Were we right to bring Mandy? She might collapse any minute. We're a long way from any hospital.'

'The most important thing at the moment,' said Delilah firmly, 'is to see a gold-crest.'

That was all the answer I was going to get, and I loved her for it, even though it made me seem a fool. I knew it meant 'I love Mandy.' (Her sudden blaze of anger yesterday proved that.) 'We have consulted fully with her doctor. We know the risks. We wouldn't have brought her today if it wasn't absolutely right. We've thought this over a dozen times. Now let's get on with living.'

We entered the wood and walked down a long ride.

'It's a matter of trust,' said Jessica, kindly trying to soften the impact of Delilah's laconic thrusts. 'The Lord is my shepherd. We read it and sing it *ad nauseam*. Now is the time to put it into action. We really have to let God take over.'

We walked on in silence—not silence, but the comforting, gentle, unobtrusive sounds of the wood. I suddenly felt the force of the word environment. What a travesty that it had become a bit of political jargon! How right it was to indicate what embraced, enclosed, enveloped us. Human tragedy was bearable sustained by this surrounding presence. What assurance of God's reality. Amazing grace. The everlasting arms. The Lord is my shepherd. The words belonged to me for the first time.

'The Lord is my shepherd.' It was some seconds before I realised that I had spoken aloud. We walked on. Moments passed.

'The Lord is my butcher,' said Delilah.

Fir trees, undergrowth, birdsong, the chequered sunlight, reeled around me. Delilah never lost her power to stagger. She was not going to let us be lulled by platitudes. But it was spoken without a hint of bitterness. Her voice was like the soft woodland noises around us, like a sigh of happy content. I had another glimpse of a rare faith that seemed to embrace life and death and everything else. But why 'butcher'?

'That's a bit paradoxical,' I murmured.

'Not really. Literal truth.'

'How come?'

'Did the Jews eat meat?'

I seemed to be back in class 1 of Delilah's school of faith.

'Yes.'

'Are there any butchers in the Bible?'

'Search me.'

'No,' put in Jessica firmly. 'Bakers, butlers and even candlestick makers, but no butchers.'

'Right. Why not?'

I thought hard. 'I suppose whoever kept the animals did the butchering too.'

'You've got it.'

'So every shepherd was a butcher as well?'

'Brilliant.'

Having got me through my eleven plus, Delilah went on to her doctoral thesis. I can't remember the details, but she quoted this and that text, with support from Jessica, and built up a total picture of God as all in all, so that even death seemed but a pause between the movements of a great symphony. Hannah's prayer, I remember, she quoted (whoever Hannah was): ' "The Lord kills and brings to life. He brings down to the grave, and up again." '

' "He forms the light, and creates darkness." Isaiah,' said Jessica.

' "The goodness and severity of God." Romans 11,' from Delilah.

' "Though he slays me, yet will I trust him." ' Jessica.

'Wouldn't some people say,' I protested mildly, 'that that is the religion of a spaniel? The more you beat it, the more devoted it gets?'

'Perhaps,' Delilah conceded. 'But it's biblical faith. It's a choice between that and Patience Strong. Total surrender to God, or sentimentality. You can't have Psalm 23 on any other terms. If you want the pastures and the still waters and the oil, it's death at the end of the line, and you've got to trust the shepherd for that too.'

And so another day had brought a packet of ideas which were too much to take in all at once. I needed time to think. Meanwhile we had turned off the ride into a clearing in the wood. We sat down on the edge of it, and for a quarter of an hour focused on this and that bird flitting in and out of the trees, passing the binoculars from one to another. I saw a jay, a spotted woodpecker, and what Delilah assured me was a tree-creeper, running up and down a treetrunk like a mouse. But we never saw a gold-crest. That would have to wait for another time.

Drama ended the day; an accident that fixed it in my mind as 'the picnic', 'that Easter Monday', which I would not forget. The Lord who was our butcher gave us a touching little reminder of our vulnerability. He was not going to let us go home without a gentle hint that he was in charge—or is my theology astray? 'Here's a little test for you,' he was saying. 'Let's see if the fine talk meant anything.

If I trip you up, will you still trust me? If I ruin your day, am I still Lord?'

It was not Mandy who collapsed. We were half way back to the others, and going down a sandy slope, when there was a sharp cry and I turned round to see Delilah full length on the ground. Delilah the poised, the athletic, the perfectly balanced, had caught her foot in a half-exposed root and gone over. She was in pain. Bruises, and a badly twisted ankle.

Jessica, efficient and practical, the Girl Guide, bandaged the ankle with a handkerchief, and we then got her standing, and with her arms round our shoulders we eventually got her back to the others. It was the first time I had been in physical contact with Delilah. It felt like a kind of privilege. Just then God didn't have anything to apologise for. He had made my day, not ruined it. My body tingled against the coolness of hers. A word kept occurring to me, a word that seemed obtrusive and out of place, a word that puzzled me with its incongruity and yet insistently described this beautiful creature. It was the word holy.

It was hot work on that sunny afternoon, and I was glad when we finally came within sight of the others, and Sebastian came to help. All the same, I was amazed at how light she was. The phrase 'My yoke is easy and my burden light' went through my mind; Matthew's gospel somewhere. But of course I was misapplying it.

Together we got Delilah back to the cars, the awkward walk enlivened by Sebastian's witticisms.

'I expect she did it on purpose. Angling for sympathy. Jason, you don't appreciate our Del enough. She feasts on admiration.' Rather obtuse of him, considering I was ready to worship her. And with that we got back to the cars. Delilah was made comfortable on the back seat with cushions and sweaters, her foot up on the seat.

'It's a good thing you've got a sense of humour,' said Sebastian as he tucked her in, and helped Mandy into the front seat.

'I haven't got a sense of humour,' said Delilah surprisingly, looking like the arrival of the Queen of Sheba. 'It's you who have the sense of humour.'

'Oh. And what is it you've got, then?'

Delilah looked at him as if seeing, through a glass door, Ciceronian sentences cut in marble.

'I have a sense of style.'

'Ah. You're perfect,' said Sebastian serenely. But she had an answer even to that.

'Don't you admire perfection?'

He shut the car door. It's funny how D. H. can say things that would seem ridiculous vanity in other people, but for her they are only right and natural. It rather shatters my view of Christian humility. I shall have to think it over.

Sebastian was driving the two of them, and I was going back with Jessica. Seb whispered to me before he got in, 'I recommend Judges 16:4. A most interesting text.'

'Judges? What judges?'

'It's a book of the Bible, you may recall. The Book of Judges. Remember, chapter 16, verse 4.'

I couldn't get used to this strange way of talking in biblical code. But I remembered the reference. Perhaps it was something about humour. Or humility.

We drove home without incident, and after making sure Mandy and Delilah were as comfortable as possible I went back to my digs.

For a long time I sat staring at my open Bible. What on earth was Sebastian thinking? What had I done, or said? How could I have given the impression that...? How could anyone else know what I...? And what in fact was happening to me?

Judges 16:4 read, 'After this, Samson fell in love with a woman named Delilah.'

8

Harvey

So ended the happiest Easter of my life. The sense of well-being survived the return to work. I almost made a fool of myself by smiling at everybody on the 7.50 on Tuesday morning. This new gift, whatever it was, was not a bank holiday jamboree. It was as solid as a child's birthday present, a pair of roller skates, a bicycle—loved and fondled and admired at the party, but needing to be tested in the real world outside. If God was Lord of life and death and cancer and the cosmos, he could certainly handle British Rail and the F.T.

'My shepherd,' I kept repeating. 'My shepherd.' I was in danger of saying it aloud. And then, mulling over that mysterious interpretation: 'My butcher.' And the personal emphasis did not seem in the least self-centred. I almost felt the mouthpiece of every fellow-traveller, as if I was praying it for them, feeling it for them, willing it for them. Delilah's wisdom haunted me: if you really love God, then the only thing that matters is people.

The dingy station, the dirty London streets, shone with a subtle radiance. Everything was all right. Everything was *safe*. Planet earth was not out of control. The depressed City faces could not depress me. The news headlines had no power to shake the orderly progress of the universe. No disaster was hopeless, no situation irredeemable.

Somehow I got through a morning's work without anyone in the office asking what had happened to me. Despite my buoyant mood I was able to tackle Endorsements concerning Hire Purchase and Leasing Agreements, General Condition 6 Cancellation Procedure, and Avoidance of Terms and Rights of Recovery, as if they were the only thing that mattered, and cleared half the backlog on my desk by lunchtime. I then went out to a rather scruffy little place in Leadenhall Market where I often ate, and there encountered Harvey. I suddenly had to think very hard.

Harvey and I had been friends on and off since school. We were never on intimate terms, but had always been completely at ease together, and more or less took each other for granted. I enjoyed a meal and a chat with him, we discussed the news, moaned about our respective offices and impossible colleagues, and bought each other drinks. Now, things had changed, and I realised the change was not in him but in me, and for the first time I felt unsure of my ground. I knew it was something to do with Delilah; but I certainly wasn't going to discuss Delilah with him.

I also felt distanced from him because I had begun to see things from a Christian angle. I could no longer be content with his easy rejection of belief.

This was another cruel paradox into which I felt trapped. 'Reach out to people,' God was saying. 'Love them as I love them.' And then, 'You're nowhere near them. You're a Christian now.' How could I work this one out? Why me?

We got through lunch with chit-chat about inflation, the performance of the pound against the deutschmark, and Arsenal's position in the league. Over coffee Harvey, without warning, said, 'Brought your Bible along with you today?'

He said it without cynicism, as if he was just interested. The funny thing was, I really wished I had. The question immediately recalled Delilah's querky but courageous habit of carrying hers everywhere, and perhaps Harvey was measuring me up against her.

'No. But at least I read it this morning.' Which was true. I was still going through Matthew's Gospel bit by bit.

'You should try it sometime,' I ventured.

'I think I'll stick to *The Times*, thanks,' he smiled. 'The world of hard facts is good enough for me.'

Surely he had played into my hands there. I tried to think of something really cutting to say. Delilah would have made mincemeat of him. I merely remarked, 'That shows a very touching faith in the media, Harvey. Hard facts? Hm. I wouldn't think of the papers quite like that.'

'Well, you know what I mean,' he justified himself. 'Of course there's a human error factor. Everyone makes mistakes sometimes. But at least they are concerned to get at the facts.'

'Human error, and human bias.'

He admitted this. 'But we're still dealing with a

basis of fact. They are concerned to report what actually happened. The Bible may be spiritually enlightening, but it's all myth.'

The mantle of Delilah seemed to have fallen on me.

'Like the *Domesday Book*, and all that stuff?' I sipped my coffee innocently. Not bad for a beginner, I thought.

Harvey lit a cigarette, and nearly fell into the trap.

'Yes, like all that stuff,' he said airily. 'I mean no, not like *Domesday Book*. *Domesday Book* is based on meticulous research. It is a wholly reliable account of the state of England at the time. It is solid historical record. Nothing could be more different.'

Well, he ought to know. I mean, Harvey is an estate agent. But the game was going my way.

'I've got news for you, Harvey.' I sounded absurdly confident, but one thing I had got from reading the commentary on Matthew's Gospel was how reliable the manuscripts were. 'The Gospels are just the same. Solid historical record. I've been into it.'

'Then why such a lot of fantasy? Why all the miraculous stuff?'

'Because it happened, I suppose.'

'But it's all fiction. Everyone knows that Jesus is a myth. It may be an inspiring story, but it's still myth. Jesus may never have existed as a historical character.'

'Like Julius Caesar, and all those chaps?' I put in innocently. I could just imagine Delilah saying it.

Harvey eyed me narrowly through a cloud of smoke. His cynical smile cut through what I thought was rather a subtle approach.

'No, not like Julius Caesar. Definitely not. There's a world of difference.' He stubbed out his cigarette and got up. 'Must go. I've got to show a client a place in Upper Norwood. We must continue this discussion another time.' His entrenched scepticism was obviously intact. I was surprised Delilah had not got through to him yet. We parted.

I clearly needed some more lessons in the Hewit School of Christian Apologetics. I thought Julius Caesar might have scored a point. I had learned that in fact the evidence for the life of J. C. Superstar was just as reliable as the evidence for the life of J. C., Roman Dictator. Anyway, I was not entirely dissatisfied with myself. I had spoken a word on behalf of my new-found faith, and I reflected that a few weeks ago I would have taken a very different line, uneasy with Delilah and her certainties, and not attempting to challenge Harvey.

That evening I was visiting the sick again, though I was careful not to take either grapes or flowers. I did however take one or two novels and some music cassettes, as Delilah was off work for a few days to rest her ankle. Mandy had been back at work, and was apparently well. Delilah was not bored. She was getting plenty of visitors. We chatted over the picnic, and enjoyed it again in retrospect. Delilah talked about birds, and went through her list of species seen and heard that day. She showed me her collection of bird books, and lent me one.

I told her of my encounter with Harvey. She laughed.

'I did my best,' I said. 'I really am convinced now that the Gospels are reliable history, and I tried to get it across. But Harvey seems to have some sort of mental blockage. He has all sorts of intellectual doubts and hang-ups.'

She laughed again. 'Intellectual doubts, is it? I wouldn't have thought that was Harvey's main problem.'

'Oh? Then what is?'

'He's lazy.'

'Lazy?' I suddenly felt like springing to Harvey's defence. He worked hard at his job, as I did. He was conscientious. He did hours of overtime. We led much the same lifestyle. If he was lazy, then I was lazy.

'It's usually laziness that keeps people from Christian commitment. Laziness, or greed. Or both. It's the moral challenge that they don't like. So-called intellectual doubts are a convenient excuse for not getting involved. Jesus didn't say, "Believe in the Athanasian Creed and follow me." He said, "Take up your cross and follow me." That's what people can't take.'

Once again Delilah had given me something to take away and ponder. Was it true? Was Harvey lazy? Was I? And if so, were we hypocrites? I suddenly remembered an early encounter with Delilah, when I had said, 'Most people who go to church are hypocrites.' My perspective had changed somewhat. I would now say 'some', not 'most'. But was Delilah hinting that in fact the opposite was true? That most people who didn't go to church were hypocrites? It was a disturbing thought.

'Thanks for the books and tapes, Jason,' she said, as I got up to go. 'That was sweet of you. I'll really enjoy them. Anyway, I should be back at work in a day or two.'

As before, I left with mixed feelings. This creature was tantalising, attractive, provocative; so close, yet out of reach; so warm, but icily rational. She was good to be with. She was more alive than most people. But oh, how dangerous to personal dignity! How destructive of all pretence!

At the door I met Jessica coming in.

'How's the patient?' she said cheerfully.

'Unsquashable. I thought that fall might have softened the brain just a little, but not a bit of it. Full of the joy of battle as usual.'

'So it's you who feel a bit bruised? Good old Delilah! And how's the ankle?'

'Doing nicely, she says. She should be able to walk in a day or two.'

'I'll give it some physio,' said Jessica. 'I've had some training. I look after the school hockey team.'

'Give it a nice hard squeeze from me, won't you?'

'Right. Yes. I will.' She smiled at me in a slightly meaningful way. 'Thanks for helping yesterday. Very good of you to help carry her.'

The feeling of Delilah's body against mine came rushing back. I blushed, I admit it.

'No trouble. Glad to help. But she's so light. I was amazed how light she was.'

'Well, she would be,' said the fairly hefty Jessica. 'She's always pretty trim. But she didn't eat much last week. She must have actually lost a pound or two.'

I was intrigued. 'Why on earth should Delilah slim? She always seems to me in such good shape.'

Jessica said very quietly, 'Well, a group from the church spent most of last week fasting and praying. Praying for Mandy, you know.'

And she added almost apologetically, 'We really do believe that prayer makes a difference. Bye now. See you.'

She went in. I was left on the doorstep. My God, these Christians! They really did amaze me. I had never met such total commitment. And yet Delilah appeared to glide through life like a debutante through a summer season, with style and lightness of touch. Here was me, thinking she was a bit of a gourmet, Delilah, for all her neat figure, a lover of the things of the flesh; her chocolate eclairs, her pavlova, her Easter eggs... Delilah fasting for a week for the sake of a friend! Though I was bound to question whether it did the slightest good, I had to admire such devotion. Here was love in action. And it made me see how completely self-centred so far were my own faltering steps in the direction of faith.

I was away the following weekend and missed church, but had another encounter with Delilah on Monday. I met Harvey for lunch again in a pub.

'How's the pilgrim's progress?' he inquired.

'Rather heavy going at present,' I had to admit, 'but still pressing on.'

'Vanity Fair getting the better of you?' He glanced around the crowded bar. 'Or has Giant Despair been knocking you about a bit?'

'Not as bad as that. Just the Hill Difficulty, I suppose.'

'Or the Delectable Mountains?'

We smiled at each other rather grimly, as Tweedledum and Tweedledee might have smiled when they agreed to have a battle. We both knew what image the word delectable conjured up. A delectable female figure who held us both on the end of a string. We were like two disabled runners in the London marathon, companions yet rivals, neither with any hope of winning.

'May I join you?'

A delectable female figure was beside us. The pub was transformed from a battleground to a temple. Delilah sat down with her ploughman's and cider. Heads turned towards our table.

'Delilah!' A glow of absurd pleasure was followed by a glow of absurd rage. She had sat down on Harvey's side of the table. Delilah alone—an unmixed joy. Delilah with Harvey—not a recipe for bliss.

'How's our ankle, then?' said Harvey. I resented his tone. As if he owned it.

'Still very tender,' said Delilah. 'Painful at times. But I'm managing. Walking is a bit slow.'

'No need to go by train,' said Harvey. 'I'll drive you up tomorrow. Then I could drop you right at the office.'

'That's very kind, Harvey, thanks, but I'll be all right. A little walking is good for it.'

Harvey snubbed. I cheered up a little.

'Funny we haven't met here before,' I said. 'Do you actually work near here?'

'Pretty near. It's in Lower Thames Street.'

Lower Thames Street. It didn't sound very salubrious to me. So it wasn't Lloyds, or the Bank, or the Stock Exchange. Lower Thames Street—that was where Billingsgate was. Good heavens, don't say she worked at Billingsgate?

'Don't say you work at Billingsgate?'

'No—but why not, if I wanted to? No, it's quite

near there. It's only a small business.' She named a
firm I had not heard of. 'Import and export.'

'The chancellor relies on our Delilah to keep the
balance of payments right,' said Harvey with heavy-
handed humour.

'Are you actually...do you...are you a director?'
I floundered. Delilah's maturity and poise, besides
her acute mind, pointed to some entrepreneurial
role.

'Good heavens, no. Give us a chance. I'm a secretary.'

Delilah was a secretary. I don't know why I
should have received the information with such total
astonishment, but it was something I had never conceived. I had imagined those delicate fingers shaking
hands with City magnates, designing, directing,
creating...but never on the keys of a typewriter.

'You mean you type?' I said rather ungraciously.

'Mostly computer work.'

'Oh. It doesn't sound very exciting.'

'No, it isn't. Hardly ever. Does work have to be
exciting?'

'Er, no, I suppose not. But I thought...I mean, I
imagined you were doing something...something
more...well, I don't know...'

'Something really important?' Delilah helped me
out. 'Like your work?'

'Yes. No! My work isn't specially important.' I
thought it as well to be modest, though my job is of
considerable importance. And I do it well.

' "Who sweeps a room..." ' murmured Delilah
over her cheese and pickles.

'I beg your pardon?'

'I said, "Who sweeps a room".'

'What? I don't know. Who does sweep a room?'

'It's a hymn,' she explained. And she quoted,

'A servant with this clause
    Makes drudgery divine,
Who sweeps a room, as for thy laws,
    Makes that and the action fine.

That's my philosophy of work.'

Stern puritan stuff. I could quite see that Delilah sweeping a room, or Delilah doing anything else, would make drudgery divine, but I hoped the conversation wasn't going to become too theological. We didn't want to upset the patrons of the Lamb and Flag. I was afraid Delilah was going to produce her Bible from her handbag. Mentally, she did. She quoted again, ' "Whatever you do, do it with all your heart, as to the Lord, and not for men." '

'I hope your boss shares your philosophy,' grinned Harvey, draining his glass. 'He might be under the strange illusion that you are supposed to be working for him.'

'No problem.' Delilah was not thrown by this. 'Of course I am working for him. It's "*as to* the Lord". It's a mental attitude.'

'Ah, that's just it,' said Harvey, lighting up, and surrounding himself with a cloud of smoke. 'This faith business. It's all in the mind.'

'Of course it's in the mind,' returned Delilah coolly. 'The most important place it could possibly be. Where else?'

I was irritated with Harvey. He hogged the conversation, he puffed smoke in our faces, and was rude to Delilah.

'Do you have to smoke, Harvey? Not very polite to Delilah. You didn't even ask her.'

'Oh Del doesn't mind, do you, darling? She likes it.'

My temperature rose. Could anything be more vulgar than calling people *darling*? And how did he know every detail of what she liked and disliked? What intimacies had gone on between them in the wilds of Lincolnshire?

'Here, have one.' He handed his packet to her. He didn't offer one to me. Not that I would have taken one, of course. But—worse and worse—Delilah did. And smoked it right through, with obvious enjoyment. Really, she is a complete enigma.

'Work,' she resumed the theme. 'It's a funny thing. Does it really matter what we do? Here's Jason worrying over indemnities and third party risks, and you're concerned about south facing aspects and main drainage and gazumping, and I'm toiling away with bills of lading and import duty, and there's the Queen opening things all day. It's all equally important. Or unimportant.'

'But we're not going to be doing the same thing all our lives,' said Harvey firmly. 'This is only a first step. The purpose of life is to get on.'

'The purpose of life is to live,' said Delilah. That rang true, because she demonstrated it in all she was and did. She was simply more alive than anyone else.

'Life at present is only endurable if you're going somewhere,' said Harvey. His commonplace mind could not appreciate Delilah's delicate wisdom. 'I mean to get on. That's my incentive. Life's too dull without it.'

Delilah watched her smoke curling upwards and gazed through it, as if seeing something beyond. She murmured quietly.

'This life's too dull without.'

'Without what?' I enquired.

'Without a cigarette, of course.' Harvey, the perfect cynic.

' "I must have God; this life's too dull without," ' Delilah mused.

I detected the rhythm of a quotation.

'Who said that?' I was curious to know.

'Another hymn?' suggested Harvey.

'Not exactly. A poem. By Studdert-Kennedy. He was chaplain in the First World War. After the war he was vicar of a church just round the corner from here. I go in there sometimes to be quiet in the lunch hour. You know, Woodbine Willie.'

'Ah, I knew cigarettes came into it somewhere.'

'He was talking about God.' Delilah was firm but patient.

'I wouldn't have said the First World War was *dull*,' said Harvey.

'Probably a lot duller than we think. War has its boredom as well as its horror. The point is, he had experienced everything, good and bad, and he still found life impossibly dull without God.'

I thought this might really get to Harvey, because I knew that despite his work and ambition, he suffered from a deep underlying ennui, and must be looking for answers, even if he didn't admit it. But he was unmoved.

'The trouble with you born-again Christians is that you are only concerned with your own needs. You find a gap in yourselves, and you invent God to fill it.'

'Not invent. Discover. Like Pluto.'

'Pluto?' I was getting left behind in this conversation. I could only think of a large floppy dog. That couldn't be it.

'Pluto?'

'This moron apparently hasn't heard of Pluto,' said Harvey. 'It happens to be one of the nine planets.'

'Of course I know that,' I returned. 'But I don't quite see...'

I am sure Harvey didn't either, but he was too cunning to admit it.

'Nobody invented Pluto,' explained Delilah. 'Somebody discovered it. In about 1930, was it? But of course it was there all the time. We don't *invent* God.'

'Better not invent *or* discover him,' said Harvey, and there was a new note of bitterness in his voice. 'Life is quite bloody enough, without having to try and explain where a God of love fits in.'

I could see we were getting into deep waters. But Delilah was a strong swimmer. She lent back with a patient sigh.

'I suppose you're going to talk about a God of love and a world of suffering,' she said, with an air of having met and answered this objection many times before.

Harvey blundered on, missing the hint of déjà vu in her tone. Poor Harvey!

'Yes, exactly. You can't reconcile a God of love and a world of suffering. It's quite illogical.'

'And I can't stand breakfast,' said Delilah.

'Breakfast?'

'Yes. It's all cold tea and burnt toast.'

'What are you getting at?'

'Don't you ever burn the toast?'

'No.' Harvey refused to admit such inefficiency. Then, under the X-ray of Delilah's gaze, added, 'Well, not normally. I may have done once.'

'Right. So how can you face breakfast, morning after morning?'

Harvey looked at me and grinned.

'You know my methods, Watson. Apply them.'

I had to admit that I too was baffled by Delilah's weird analogy.

' "A God of love and a world of suffering." ' Sherlock Holmes enlightened us. 'It's such a ridiculous phrase. Totally out of proportion. Both halves are false. "A God of love"—as if that was all there was to be said about God. Minimising him. Ignoring all the other things that are true of him: God of power, justice, judgement, wrath, holiness, truth...'

'Where does the toast come in?' asked Harvey meekly.

'I should have thought it was obvious. You burn the toast once, it doesn't put you off breakfast for life. You don't talk about "a breakfast of burnt toast". You don't get things so completely out of proportion.'

'But you have to admit suffering is pretty universal.' For answer Delilah glanced round the bar. A crowd of lively, well-dressed, well-fed, talking, laughing, joking, smoking, drinking people. A general air of good fellowship, wealth and prosperity.

'I don't forget the suffering,' she said quietly. We knew it was true. Mandy was never out of her thoughts. She had fasted for a week. And she was well to the fore in St Paul's involvement in all kinds of caring concerns.

'It's just the phrase "a world of suffering" that is wide of the mark. As if it wasn't also a world of enormous wealth of resources, fantastic beauty, physical pleasure, creativity, friendship, joy.... I wouldn't talk about "a world of happiness" but it's equally unrealistic to talk about "a world of suffering".'

We got up to go.

'You've got a point there, Del,' said Harvey generously. 'I'll have to think about it. Just now, I've got a world of clients lining up to see me.' He paid for himself and for Delilah. Not for me. 'Two, to be precise. Farewell, my lovely.'

For one horrible moment I thought he was going to kiss her.

He rushed away.

'Nice seeing you, Jason,' said Delilah. 'Perhaps we'll meet again here.'

'Yes, fine. I'd no idea you worked so near. How come we never meet on the train?'

'I usually go on the early one. The 7.41.'

She limped out of the pub.

'Can I give you a hand?' Delilah, lame, looked so deliciously helpable.

'No thanks. I've got to stand on my own two feet. Walking on my own is good for it. Part of the physiotherapy.'

'Yes, right. Well, go carefully.'

'I will. See you at St Paul's on Sunday.'

'Yes. Er, well, I'm not sure. I've got an awful lot to do. I may not be able to make it.'

'Priorities, Jason. First things first. One hour out of a hundred and sixty-eight. Remember your promise.'

'Yes, right. I expect I'll be there.' In fact I really enjoyed going, and was looking forward to it; but I did not want to be pressured. I gave myself the loophole.

'But of course it's only for a trial period! That's what I said.'

We parted on the corner of Lime Street. She smiled.

'It's the same for all of us. The trial ends with death. Then the real living starts.'

She limped away towards the river.

9

Mars Bars

'All authority is given to me,' Graham was saying. I woke up with a start from the semi-attentive doze which even the best of sermons are apt to induce. Especially for those like myself who have been working overtime all through the week.

All authority? It sounded a bit megalomaniac to me. Was this the recipe for a healthy church? Graham wasn't the autocratic type anyway. I must have missed the point. Luckily (as preachers often do) he repeated himself.

' "All authority is given to me," Jesus says in the closing words of Matthew's Gospel.' Ah, Matthew's Gospel. I felt more at home, although this was a bit I hadn't got to yet in my reading. I had got rather bogged down in chapter 24.

'Now, he's not being megalomaniac,' said Graham, echoing my thoughts. 'Jesus makes these staggering claims, and yet his lifestyle is totally simple and totally humble. He's not some kind of Hitler or Mussolini. He doesn't say he *has* authority. He says it has been *given* him by his Father. He has been entrusted with it.'

His gaze swept round the church, as if to involve everyone in what he wanted to say.

'Now here comes the interesting bit,' he went on. 'This is where we come in. Jesus has this authority, and what does he do with it? Just what you good executives do at work, I'm sure.' (I expect he was thinking 'You yuppies', but he was too polite to say it.) 'He delegates it!'

Having asked a rhetorical question, he now asked a real one. Graham has this slightly embarrassing habit of getting people to respond during a sermon. I suppose it keeps people awake, but it reminds me uncomfortably of school, and the feeling of not having done my homework.

'What have we just been singing?' he asked.

'Majesty,' piped up some precocious disciple.

'That's right. And what did we sing? "Majesty, kingdom authority…" ' and several voices chimed in, ' "Flows from his throne, unto his own, his anthem raise." '

'That's it. We'll forget about the anthem for the moment. I'm sure the choir has got something good for us later on!' (I can't get used to this attitude to worship as a kind of cabaret.) 'God's authority flows from his throne unto his own—to his own people. That's us. He delegates his authority to us. So after the bit about authority comes the challenge: "Therefore go and make disciples of all nations." We have the authority and we have the command. What are we doing about it?'

I had to admit all sorts of giants and dragons sprang out of hiding when he said this. Aggressive

evangelists, mindless preachers, insensitive mission-
aries, American TV religion, gospel tracts, crusades
in football stadiums, arrogant denial of other
faiths... I must say I find the whole missionary thing
hard to take, and I had to ask whether Graham,
much as I admired him, was living in the real world.
More questions for Delilah afterwards.

Graham went on to apply the message to St
Paul's.

'I believe Jesus is calling us into the same pattern.
He called his disciples to be with him for a period of
learning and training. Then he sent them out. That's
what we are doing. I hope we are doing it all the
time. But we're doing it in a special way this summer. SPACE, and the Mission. The SPACE weekend
is for us to get to know Jesus better, and get to know
each other better. It will be a time of receiving his
authority. Claiming his promises. Accepting his
power. Then the mission in July will be a special
time of going out with the message. "Go and make
disciples of all nations." '

And he went on to outline detailed plans for
SPACE and the Mission.

We had coffee together after the service as usual. I
was beginning to wonder if St Paul's was the right
place for me after all. And yet I felt thoroughly
involved. The phrase 'only for a trial period' stuck in
the back of my mind as an escape hatch, though it
was becoming less important. Paradoxically, with all
my doubts, questions and criticisms of St Paul's, this
was where I felt at home. I fetched coffee for Mandy
and Delilah.

Sebastian accepted the idea of the Mission in his

usual unthinking way. All he was worried about was a title.

'We really must have a zippy title,' he began. 'Parish Mission is just too boring. It's a complete turn-off. I have some great ideas. I think I'll suggest them to Graham. SPICE, for example. St Paul's In Conflict with Everybody. That should bring 'em in.'

Mandy laughed happily. She was looking relaxed and remarkably well. I thanked God inwardly. No one knew what lay ahead for her, or how soon things might change, but for the moment she was alive, working, at peace, enjoying every moment. Surely that was a great gift. Whether that week of fasting had anything to do with it was another matter, but I saw her, frail and precarious, as an answered prayer, and I was thankful.

'SPADE,' said Sebastian. 'Let's call a spade a spade. St Paul's Answer to Doubts about Everything. Or SPORT. St Paul's Orgy of Ranting and Tub-thumping. Rather good, that. Graham will like it.'

'NUT,' said Jessica, not to be outdone. 'Negligible Untutored Twit.'

Sebastian was used to receiving insults. He simply returned them.

'NUT. That's your union isn't it? N.U.T. National Union of Troublemakers.'

'Libel,' returned Jessica. 'We work twice as hard as you nine-to-five layabouts. We are dedicated to our job. Anyway, I'm not a member of the N.U.T.'

'No, of course not,' Sebastian mocked on. 'So degrading. After all, we're Christian, aren't we? Much too middle class and respectable for that sort of thing. Wouldn't soil our dainty little fingers....'

He looked pointedly at Jessica's rather hamfisted hands on the table.

'Time,' called Delilah decisively. 'End of round one, thank you. The point is, what are we going to do about the Mission? That's more important than what it's called.'

This was my cue.

'I'm afraid my question is not how, but why. All you lot are happy with the idea of a mission, but I haven't got over the first hurdle.'

'BATSO,' said Sebastian, whose mental growth seemed to have graduated from jokes to acronyms. 'Back to Square One, first principles. Quite right.'

'I should have thought that's what the sermon was about,' said Jessica.

'I'm not convinced. Isn't it an outmoded concept? Is it realistic to go down the High Street and proclaim our faith?'

'Realism itself.' Delilah as usual was quietly uncompromising. She at least, and everything about her, was totally real.

'But surely the important thing,' I persisted, like Daniel putting his head a little nearer to the lions, 'is to accept the faith in ourselves, and to live it out?'

Jessica decided it was time for her church history lesson.

'What if Augustine had said that?'

'Augustine?'

'St Augustine. Sixth century AD. He brought the gospel to England, you know.'

'Yes, well, fine, but that was a long time ago. We're living in the 1990s. It's a different world.'

This seemed to trigger off a spring in Jessica. I

could see her mentally drumming her chalk on the blackboard. Class Three trembled.

'Fallacy!' she pronounced. 'Heresy, I might almost say! Popular misconception Number One. It's a complete misunderstanding.' The National Executive of the N.U.T. could be thankful she was not a member, I reflected. She would have given them a rough ride. 'It's the *same* world,' she went on. 'The same planet earth. The same physical laws at work, the same moral principles at stake, the same human nature, the same questions, and the same answer! Nothing has changed. Some of the furniture has been rearranged. That's all.'

'Yes, miss,' I nearly said. If she had told me to write out a hundred times 'Nothing has changed,' I would probably have done it. All authority, just at that moment, seemed to be given to Jessica. I tried to rally my defences.

'All right, I agree that Augustine was a Good Thing—though surely if he hadn't come, the gospel would have reached us in some other way? Anyway, I still don't think we have the right to force our religion down other people's throats.'

Delilah laughed. Rather irritating, as I was pursuing a most important subject; it was something I really wanted to thrash out, and it wasn't very pleasant to be lectured by one girl and laughed at by another. Then she came out with one of her superb *non sequiturs*.

'Like Mars Bars?'

Why was it Delilah's polemics always seemed to be associated with chocolate in my mind?

'Mars Bars?'

'Mars Bars,' put in Sebastian. 'That sums it up

very neatly. The wit and wisdom of Ms D. He-wit.
Excuse the sexist language. She-wit. Mars Bars. The
French have a word for it, you know. *L'ésprit d'escal-
ier.*'

He really hadn't a clue what she was talking
about, and I hadn't a clue what he was talking
about, so confusion reigned.

'Lay spree de what?'

'*L'ésprit d'escalier*. A very subtle phrase. Untransla-
table. Staircase wit. It means the witty retort you
wished you had thought of at the time. You only
think of it when going down the steps. When it's too
late. Our Del is rather good at it. And she doesn't
wait till the stairs.'

That at least was clear enough, and quite sensible,
coming from Sebastian. It certainly described
Delilah's method to a T. She was a master of retort.
Mistress. No—dash it, master. Does everything
have to be non-sexist language? We don't talk about
a Mistress of Arts, or a Spinster of Arts, for that
matter. I jerked my mind back into the groove.

'Yes, well, we were talking about Mars Bars. At
least our guru was. Guru-ess.' I thought Sebastian
would enjoy my little joke. He did, and of course he
had to come back with another.

'There's this kid in our office who is always raving
about sexist language. I caught her out once. It's
impossible to talk to her, as all through the lunch
hour she's plugged into this Walkman thing. I
shouted at her, "Jennifer, will you please switch off
that infernal machine so that we can have a straight
talk, man to man." She fell straight into the trap. She
said, "It's not an infernal machine, it's a Walkman,
and will you please cut out the chauvinist language."

"So sorry," I said. "I'll try again. Will you please switch off that Walkperson!" '

The company tittered dutifully.

'Mars Bars,' I said sternly. I was not going to be diverted again.

'I think it's a shame,' said Delilah, as if the interruptions had never taken place, 'how parents give their children Mars Bars. They've no right to do it. It's cruel. The NSPCC should be informed.'

Here we go again, I thought. We'll have to humour her. No doubt there's a sting in the tail coming. But I still couldn't quite see the connection.

'Forcing Mars Bars down children's throats. They are quite happy with stew and rice pudding.'

I began to see what she was getting at. Then she moved into forward gear.

'Good heavens, Jason, if *you* haven't seen it, then what hope for anyone? Don't you feel that you've found something supremely wonderful? It's so recent! Isn't the taste of it fresh in your mouth?'

' "Now that you have tasted that the Lord is good",' put in Sebastian automatically. '1 Peter 2:3.'

'My name isn't Peter,' I said distractedly. 'And what's all this about 1−2−3?'

'Dear idiot,' said Sebastian. 'The first epistle of St Peter, chapter 2, verse 3. Still, perhaps we can't expect too much at this stage. You're still like a newborn babe.'

'What's that?' I retorted sarcastically. '1 Peter 2:4, I suppose.'

'No, 2:2, actually,' he grinned in triumph. Who needs a Bible when they have got Sebastian? But he must have been bluffing. I'll have to look it up. One day I'll—

'Anyway,' cut in Delilah, finishing her coffee, 'that's my motive for mission. What God offers us is something so marvellous, all we need to do is to help people to see it, then there will be no stopping them. You don't have to persuade a normal healthy child to like Mars Bars!'

'Well, I see that. If that's what a mission is, then perhaps I can go along with it. There's no need to mount a crusade against poor defenceless little me! After all I'm only a newborn babe. So I'm told.'

'I was only crusading against that ridiculous phrase,' said Delilah demurely.

'Phrase? What phrase?'

'You said something about forcing religion down people's throats.'

'Well?'

'Two objections. First...'

I seemed to be in the headmaster's office again. Headmistress's. Headteacher's.

'First, it's a horrible platitude. I really don't know where you get your language from! One thing that's worth learning about being a Christian is not to use other people's worn-out language. "If anyone is in Christ he is a new creation." '

Sebastian, who was scribbling something on a piece of paper, looked up to say '2 Corinthians 5:15.'

'Being a new creation involves using words freshly,' she flowed on as if she had not heard... 'No more platitudes. Other people's thrown-away phrases. It's like a tramp picking up cigarette ends. Seventeen actually.'

'Er? Seventeen fag-ends?'

'I was talking to Sebastian. 5:17.'

'Oh yes. 2 Corinthians 5:17. I must remember that one. And the other objection?'

'Ah, yes. I'm afraid it's you who's not living in the real world this time, Jason. People don't force religion down people's throats these days. Nobody! Pentecostalists or Baptists or Mormons or Jehovah's Witnesses or Buddhists or Muslims...they just don't do it. The hard sell is totally out. Perhaps you hadn't noticed? So why would you expect a parish church to do it? You are at least a hundred years out of date.'

I was against the ropes, and I was thinking it was time the referee stopped the fight, when I was saved by the bell, in the shape of a triumphant bellow from Sebastian.

'Got it!' he cried, holding up his bit of paper. 'MARS BARS. The ideal title! Listen. "Mission Actually Restores the Soul. Believe in A Risen Saviour." Isn't that great? And there are all sorts of variations. "Make A Radical Start. Become A Real Saint." I might come up with something even better. I'll go and talk to Graham straight away!'

And he actually went.

' "You suffer fools gladly since you yourselves are wise",' said Jessica drily, which I thought was rather hard.

I must say one thing for Sebastian. He does make an effort to use words freshly. I mean, he's not content with platitudes.

10

Sin

I was still uneasy. 'Mission' and 'evangelism' were hitherto almost completely negative words for me; I had a lot of fears and doubts to overcome. I had so lately been in the shoes of the evangelised. Now I was lining up on the side of the evangelists, and it took some getting used to. Could we really set about preaching the gospel with the same sublime single-mindedness of the Galilean peasants in the ancient world? Was Jessica right? Was the world still basically the same? Was the good news just as good? And good in the same way?

'It's the truth,' was Delilah's answer. For her, that settled it. She was certainly a fundamentalist—yet obviously in a different league from the kind of people who said the earth is flat, full stop. Every article of faith she appeared to have wrestled with beforehand. Every doubt and objection and criticism she seemed to have an answer for. She had battled through the turbulence and come out on top, and the cloud of faith she floated on was deceptively calm.

'There are no easy answers.' I had heard people say that so often. I had heard people say it to Delilah. I had said it myself. 'What you mean is, there are no answers,' she would reply. 'No, I didn't say that. I said there are no easy answers.' 'Ah. Then there are hard answers?' How subtly, how simply, she won her point! I could see how she exposed our shallow thinking. 'No easy answers,' was, like most platitudes, an excuse for laziness. Her mind was never lazy. She had surrendered it, dedicated it, baptised it into Christ. She loved quoting Scriptures about the mind, with or without Sebastian to give chapter and verse: 'Love the Lord your God with all your...mind;' 'Let this mind be in you which was also in Christ Jesus;' 'We have the mind of Christ.' I jotted them down to think over later.

As it happened, our debate about mission was to be continued the following Saturday. The really big question remained in my mind. I kept thinking about the Mars Bars. But what about the Bounty, Twix and Penguins that lay side by side on the shelf? What about the Smarties and Liquorice Allsorts? And all sorts was the word, what with Eastern mysticism, and meditation, and yoga, and spiritualism, and scientology, and New Age religion, besides the range of more familiar denominations and world faiths.

So I found myself drifting along to The Meeting Place in the vague hope that there might be a book that would explain it all. But was there any book not written by an insider? Weren't they all like advertisements for Mars Bars? Didn't they all claim to refresh the parts that other beers didn't reach, and ignore the claims of the others?

I went to The Meeting Place this time without

dreading meeting other people. And meet them I did. There were Mandy and Delilah, with the inevitable coffee cups in front of them, discussing the latest book they had just acquired. I recognised it as one that Graham had recommended to help people prepare for the mission. I joined them.

'Funny how the life of faith seems to be quite impossible without coffee.'

'Absolutely,' Mandy agreed.

'How have you been this week?'

'Stable, thank you, Jason. No relapses. No broken engagements. No missed concerts.'

'No concerts, either,' said Delilah. 'Strict discipline. Early bed.'

'And how's your ankle?'

'In great form. Ready to kick anyone! Nearly back to normal. We'll have another game of tennis in a week or two, right?'

'Fine. Just let me know when. I'll get myself in peak training. I'm going on a diet of Mars Bars.'

I explained what I had come for. We discussed books.

'We had a new one in the library,' said Mandy. ' "The Problem of World Religions" or some name like that. By Herbert P. Wannamaker. Very well reviewed.'

'Did you read it?'

'I read the first twenty pages.'

'Twenty pages out of…'

'About five hundred and fifty.'

'And?'

'I could put it down.' Herbert P. Wannamaker was annihilated at a stroke.

'I know a better one,' said Delilah.

'If you recommend it, I'll get it.'

'You've got it already. It's the Bible.'

Delilah, fundamentalist. *Not* very funny. I was serious.

'I'm serious, Delilah.'

'Of course. So am I. Ultimately these books tell you nothing. Much better to stick to the Bible, and make up your own mind.'

'I am a bear of very little brain when it comes to theology,' I said meekly.

'Very little is enough. In fact it's better. Children, that's what we are called to be like. Accept the kingdom of God like a little child.'

'I know I'm only a newborn babe...'

'Lucky you. So desire the pure milk of the word.'

'Milk?'

'It's how that verse Sebastian quoted goes on. "As newborn babes, desire the pure milk of the word." '

'Mars Bars, if you like,' put in Mandy. 'Made of milk chocolate. Actually, I thought that illustration Graham used on Sunday was very helpful. The one about cough mixture.'

'I don't quite remember. What was it all about? I remember him saying something about cough mixture.'

'He was talking about this very point,' Mandy explained. 'Why the Christian gospel? What about other ways of salvation? And he said, "Of course there may be good things in other religions. They may help you to be more at peace with yourself and the universe. They may help you to be a better member of the family, of society. They may bring healing. But they don't tackle the problem at the root. They are like medication, when what we need is an operation. They are like drugs which soothe and relieve pain, but they don't cut out the tumour. They are like cough mixture to a man with throat cancer." '

The word cancer came like a blow between the eyes. Yet it was Mandy who had said it, Mandy whose leukaemia had been diagnosed only weeks before. Too near the bone for her—but she related the sermon without a qualm. She was not the stiff-upper-lip type, so she must have worked through her condition, I suspect with Delilah's help, and come to a point of total acceptance.

So was that the whole picture? Was there that radical difference between our faith and others? The difference between medicine and surgery?

'Is there really all that difference?' I asked Mandy.

There was quite a pause. She looked at Delilah. Delilah stared into space. Mandy looked at me. She eventually spoke, so quietly, so thoughtfully, it was almost like talking to herself. Almost like a prayer.

'No one else died for my sins.'

The silence was like an act of worship. It was only after a long time I felt able to break it. Sin. I suppose that had to come into it somewhere. So that was the cancer at the heart of things. The poison in the blood.

'Ah. Yes. Sin. I admit it's a real factor. But aren't we a bit over-obsessed with it sometimes? Do preachers have to descant about it so much?'

'Abolish sin, abolish God,' said Delilah. 'You can't have one without the other. For the atheist, of course, there's no such thing as sin. But once you see God, you see your own sin. It's inevitable. They're related, like food and hunger.'

Mandy: 'Water and thirst.'

Delilah: 'Light and shadow.'

Mandy: 'Sleep and tiredness.'

Delilah: 'Remember Peter and Jesus in the boat?'

Me: 'Uh? Can't quite remember.'

Delilah: 'Perhaps it's not in Matthew's gospel. One of the others. Peter suddenly sees who Jesus really is, and his reaction is not, "Lord, I want to follow you, I want to be near you," but he says, "Lord, keep away from me, because I am a sinful man." If God is God, that's how it's bound to be. It's because it's the real you. Your deepest self. The worst about you. The rock bottom.' And then she produced one of her paradoxes; Oscar Wilde turned theologian.

'Only the worst is good enough for God.'

I pondered it. It rang true. Mandy followed it up with another epigram.

'I love that phrase of, who was it, Kierkegaard, wasn't it? I can't remember: "The blessedness of knowing that before God man is always in the wrong." '

'Yes, Kierkegaard,' I said pontifically. 'Kierkegaard 3:16.' Mandy laughed.

'You've never heard of Kierkegaard, have you? Admit it!'

'I admit it. Not sure I want to either.'

'But he's got a point. It's absolutely basic. We come to God as forgiven sinners. There's no other way. Any other way, we're not coming to God, only to some man-made image of God.'

'Right,' said Delilah, hammering home the point. ' "You can't know God as a friend unless you have first known him as an enemy." That's another quotation. From Luther actually. Perhaps you've heard of him?'

'Oh yes, I've heard of Luther all right. He comes in *Superman*. Lex Luther. A great guy. Did he really say that?'

I got up to go. Despite the fooling, I had got yet another packet of ideas, a new slant on the gospel, some things I felt were basic, and which I wanted to work out on my own, with the help of a Bible and a notebook. I took Delilah's advice, and left without scanning the section on comparative religion. I saw that, if the girls were right, there was the basis for the mission, and I could not hold aloof.

I did make one decision there and then. I decided to go to SPACE. If there was space. Numbers were limited, and it was only a week away. I decided to let God make the decision. If it was fully booked, then he didn't want me to go. As soon as I got home I rang Graham. No answer. I rang the mission office. No one there. Well, there wouldn't be, it was Saturday. But there was an answering machine (an odd misnomer, I've always thought; answer was the one thing it didn't do); I left my message. God's answer this time was—as so often, I was learning in the school of prayer—wait.

Graham preached the next day on prayer. He was calling everyone to pray for SPACE, and for the mission. I had noticed how things so often seemed to work together when you began to look at life with the eye of faith. And here was Graham talking about waiting with a text from the psalms. 'Wait on the Lord.' He didn't talk about answerphones, but he had an equally down-to-earth illustration, and amused us all with talk about his favourite sport. He was in a buoyant mood.

'I am not sure if there will actually be cricket in heaven. I have heard people say, "Well, if there isn't, I don't want to go there!" I am not saying positively that God is a cricketer. The biblical evidence is inconclusive. But what is certain is that God's answer to prayer is like a call in cricket. Now in fact, when you're out there in the middle, you hear all sorts of variations: "We'll take one." "Stay there." "Can you?" "I'm looking." "Your call." "One on the throw." "Come on." But really there are only three basic calls: Yes, No, or Wait. And that's how God calls to us.'

Yes, no, or wait. Even I, a mere tennis player, knew that. It was comforting to hear the complex matter of prayer reduced to this simple formula.

Graham ended with a fine passage from Isaiah, something about those who waited on the Lord mounting up with wings like eagles. There had certainly been moments during that glorious Easter week when language about eagles was not too high-flown to describe my feelings. (I had never actually seen an eagle. No doubt Delilah had. And Harvey.) But I had always regarded waiting as a negative experience. It was reassuring to know that, in the eternal perspective, waiting could be positive and creative.

'Waiting, for the batsman, can save your wicket,' Graham concluded. 'Waiting on God can save your soul.'

Our conversation afterwards was light-hearted.

'Is everyone going to SPACE?' demanded Jessica.

Interrogative, expecting the answer Yes. ('Come on girls, we're all playing hockey, aren't we?')

'Jason isn't,' said Mandy. 'He doesn't like challenge and enjoyment!'

'Just to surprise you—actually, I am. At least, I want to. I've applied. I don't know if there's still room.' I explained about the answerphone.

'You'd better go and check with Brenda now,' said Jessica. Brenda was the parish secretary, who was handling the bookings.

'Answerphones. A great invention,' said Sebastian. 'A wonderful excuse for doing nothing while appearing to be the acme of efficiency. Have you heard about the fire station at Little Snoring? They determined to be up-to-date, and have the latest equipment. They installed an answerphone.'

Amid the laughter Jessica looked puzzled. Her sense of humour is, shall we say, a little retarded. At least, when it comes to Sebastian's type of humour.

'So what? I don't get it.'

Eventually she did. 'Talking of fire,' Sebastian went on, 'I was rather surprised to see this big sign up at our local crematorium the other day.' Nothing is sacred to Sebastian if it is material for a joke. He could get a job on *Spitting Image* any day. 'I was there for my grandfather's funeral. And there was this great sign up on the wall: PLEASE DO NOT SMOKE.'

Jessica did not see the joke. Or chose not to.

'Terrible places, crematoria,' went on St Paul's resident comedian. 'They cause considerable atmospheric pollution. Shouldn't be allowed. We'll have to write to our MP. Alert Friends of the Earth.

Pollution's a big issue these days. All the schools are into it. Is yours, Jess?'

'Certainly,' replied Jessica. 'I'm actually doing a project on it in my class this term. Starting with Genesis 1.'

'Quite right,' said Sebastian solemnly. 'And don't forget the dangers of lead in the atmosphere. One school I know has started a movement called CUP.'

He waited patiently. The dramatic pause was part of the game. Sebastian knew the importance of timing. Waiting was as important in vaudeville as in theology.

'The Campaign for Unleaded Pencils.'

'We were talking about SPACE,' said Jessica, not amused. 'You were trying to get Mrs Shore to go, Delilah. Did you persuade her?'

'No, I don't think so. She's interested, and I'm sure she would enjoy it. But she says she doesn't like these guitars and things.'

Jessica smiled. 'You should have said, "All right, I'll make sure there aren't any things. Only guitars." '

'Guitars and things' was a joke between them.

'Funny how the poor innocent guitar is associated with some kind of Pentecostal knees-up. It's about the gentlest sound there is. I asked her if she'd ever heard Segovia. She hadn't, so we didn't get very far.'

'We'll lend her a record one day.'

'She obviously thinks you belong to the Monster Raving Charismatic Loony Party,' said Sebastian. 'She's thinking of electric guitars, of course.'

'Yes, and she doesn't seem to have noticed that we never have them at St Paul's. Never have had. We'll have to work on dear Mrs Shore.'

'Quite,' said Jessica. 'These people are so mindless. They just don't think. We'll put her on the prayer list.'

'Poor Mrs Shore,' Sebastian went on. 'She won't know what's hit her. The combined might of Jessica and Delilah. Onward, Christian soldiers. Soldierettes. ATS. What's the word? WRACS. Wrens. Rule, Delilah, Delilah rule the waves. Shore, anyway...' he babbled on unstoppably.

'She's another of these 1662 diehards,' said Jessica. 'The trouble is, they want the old Prayer Book for all the wrong reasons. I am a great admirer of the Prayer Book. Our guarantee of sound doctrine. But they treat it like Stonehenge or the Tower of London. A bit of English heritage.'

Mandy laughed. 'Remember Mr Bachelor? Another of the 1662 brigade.' ('Probably about when he was born,' chipped in Sebastian.) 'He's one of those stiff-upper-lip types. Like Colonel Mustard in Cluedo. And Delilah said innocently, "The 1662 Prayer Book? It's a bit *passionate*, isn't it?" '

'*La belle dame sans merci*,' said Sebastian. I don't know where he gets all this French from. ' "Let your conversation be always full of grace, seasoned with salt, so that you may know how to answer everyone." Colossians 4:6. That's the style, Del old gel. Plenty of salt.'

'Why passionate?' I asked. My knowledge of the Prayer Book, 1662 or any other date, was rudimentary.

'Well isn't it? "Lord, have mercy upon us;" "A broken and a contrite heart;" "We worship thee, we glorify thee;" "Love the Lord thy God with all thy heart." '

'Yes, I see what you mean.'

'I don't think old Bachelor did. He just couldn't see it.'

'Perhaps you'd better put him on your prayer list?' I suggested. And immediately regretted it. Prayer was not a joke.

But Delilah came to the rescue.

'Don't worry. He's on it.'

Sebastian treated us to one more comic act that morning.

'Passionate. Now why didn't I think of that? *L'esprit d'escalier.* Now my trouble is the opposite to most people's. I've got the witty answer all lined up, but nobody asks me the question. I want a feed.'

I humoured him. 'What question do you want to be asked?'

'Well, with all this talk about the Prayer Book, I thought someone would get on to the Authorised Version of the Bible.'

'Let's get on to the Authorised Version of the Bible then.'

'All right. Get on to it then.'

'I'm on it.'

'What about it?'

'Well, the Authorised Version is obviously a Good Thing. Like St Augustine.'

'But you can't make sense of it today, surely?'

'Why not? It seems pretty straightforward to me.' I really didn't know if I was just acting Mr Bachelor, and being a good feed, or speaking in my own person. I didn't have any objections to the AV myself. Perhaps I just didn't know it well enough. Anyway, Sebastian had his cue.

'Straightforward? I wouldn't say that. Suffer ye

thus far. Gird up the loins of your mind. Ye are not straitened in us, but ye are straitened in your own bowels. Wherefore speak ye leasing in your heart? What think ye? Whether of them twain will ye? Neither? I trow not. Woe worth the day! Excuse me, everybody. I must go. I'm having lunch with my parents. See you at SPACE, if not before.'

He had made a point, besides making an ass of himself. Maybe the AV was a bit obscure in places. But what idiot would spend time looking up weird phrases, stringing them together, and learning them by heart, just for the sake of a cheap laugh?

'It's a great gift,' murmured Delilah, gazing after him.

'What?' I was amazed. 'Rather second-rate, I would have thought.'

'I wasn't thinking of his clowning,' she said. 'His happiness. How many people do you know who are consistently happy? Seb is never moody, never dull, never bears a grudge, never loses his temper, is never really unkind, always cheerful.'

'Sounds a bit like 1 Corinthians 13,' said Mandy.

'You're right. Not far off. Happiness. A rare gift. A very great gift.'

I digested this. Perhaps there was more to Sebastian than I realised. Perhaps I judged him too harshly. All I knew about happiness at the moment was that, whenever Delilah was around, one was very close to it, and when she wasn't, it didn't have much meaning.

She went on. 'I have a theory about happiness. "There is no duty we neglect so much as the duty of being happy." Some literary wallah said that. It's a duty. People don't see it like that.'

'Stevenson.'

'Trust Mandy to know. Stevenson. Right. And remember that book that's been on the church book-stall for years? *The Happiest People on Earth*. You haven't got time to read all these books, but you can learn a lot just from the titles. The happiest people on earth—that's what Christians are supposed to be. And some of them are. But most of us?' She looked round the table. There was no need for anyone to answer.

'You see? We've been talking about the mission. People discuss the best methods. House meetings. Open-air meetings. Visiting. Personal counselling. Healing services.... You can go on and on. But that's all secondary. The most important thing for the evangelisation of Britain today, is for Christians to be happy, and to look happy.'

She had cast her spell. Each of us was to some extent caught up in her vision, though it was too vast to take in all at once. More food for thought. I was fairly certain, speaking personally, that if all Christians were like Delilah, and looked like Delilah, the evangelisation of Britain could be achieved in record time.

11

Kicking Away the Ladder

I went in search of Brenda. I suddenly felt unsure about SPACE. I had decided on it rather impulsively. I really needed time to be alone. To think. To pray. I was wary of more pressure. Over the last few weeks I had received a crowd of new experiences, new ideas, new thoughts, new feelings. 'If anyone is in Christ he is a new creation,' Delilah had quoted. It was joyfully, painfully, true. Life with Delilah was like being on a roller-coaster. Before you had recovered from a swerve, the next loop came. Then a climb, then a swoop. I needed a turn on the ferris wheel, to get a calmer view of things. Was SPACE what I needed? I had qualms. Wasn't it going to be high-powered training for the mission? Could I take it?

Worse than that, had I decided to go for the wrong motive? Life with Delilah—I shouldn't have said that. Life with Jesus—that's what I meant, wasn't it? A Freudian slip. My motives were only too clear: I was going because Delilah would be there. And

Harvey certainly wouldn't be.

Doubts, regrets, self-blame, crowded upon me. God could not possibly mean me to go. I was thankful that at least I had committed it to him in all honesty. If there wasn't a place for me, then that was his answer. I felt happier—though what Delilah and Mandy had been saying about sin was beginning to come home to me. It was painfully obvious now.

'Lord,' I silently prayed, 'you are in control. Thank you. Please decide. Save me from myself.'

I found Brenda in the area at the back of the church, clipboard in hand, talking to a couple. I waited. Yes, no, or wait. For the moment, wait. A brightly-coloured book on the bookstall caught my eye. *The Happiest People on Earth.* So that was it. And yet how did the happiness thing go with a consciousness of sin? Not at all clear. Wait. I waited.

I scanned the notice board. One whole section devoted to SPACE, each notice with a witty title. SPACE PROGRAMME—the timetable for the weekend. SPACE AGE—arrangements for different age groups, activities for the children. SPACE TRAVEL—those offering lifts and those wanting them. SPACE CENTRE—location and phone number of the parish office.

'Jason, I'm so glad you're still here.' Brenda was free at last. The couple moved off. 'I've been meaning to see you. I got your message last night, but it was too late to phone you then. It's great that you want to come to SPACE.'

'I'm sorry I left it so late. I expect you're fully booked already.'

'No, that's all right, we can fit you in. We're going to be pretty full. I've had five more bookings this morning. We'll be well over a hundred. But we can take you. Only I'm afraid it may mean sharing a room. I hope you don't mind?'

I could hardly back out now on such a slender pretext. Brenda gave me a leaflet with the details, and I paid a deposit.

'I'll work out the room list and let you know later in the week. All right?'

'Yes, fine. Thanks very much.'

I was in for a weekend of Challenge and Enjoyment. With a shared room. I just hoped it wasn't with Sebastian.

'The right person, Lord. Whoever you want. I don't mind. You choose. Thank you.'

I was praying about everything now, though in total ignorance of how prayer worked. I took it on trust from Graham and others that God always answered, even though it was sometimes No, or Wait. I hadn't yet worked out how this squared with the teaching of Jesus. I had an acronym embedded in my mind, picked up from one of Graham's sermons (not one of Sebastian's this time):

Ask
Seek
Knock

I had read Jesus' words in Matthew's Gospel, 'Ask, and you shall receive. Seek and you shall find. Knock, and it shall be opened.' What was the secret? The Power of Positive Thinking? Or faith? So again, there were plenty of unanswered questions. No easy answers—but, I remembered, schooled by Delilah, that doesn't mean no answers at all. I simply left the rationale to be worked out later, and launched into the adventure of prayer. It was like pushing a boat out. I had no idea where I would end up, but at least I was afloat. It was more a matter of trusting than asking.

So God wanted me to go to SPACE. With an effort I accepted it, and then put it out of my mind for the week. Work absorbed me. Only one incident in the week reminded me of it. Delilah and Harvey and I met once more for lunch in the pub.

Harvey sipped his Guinness.

'Are you ready to fix dates for Scotland yet?' he asked Delilah.

Scotland? What was all this about?

'Yes, I think so. When were you thinking of?'

'July, sometime,' said Harvey.

'Not ideal. We have this mission, you know.'

'Mission? Oh yes, your mission. You wouldn't like to give it a miss?'

'No, Harvey.'

'No. Right. So when is it?'

'The third week in July.'

'Well, then, we could go away after that.'

'Sorry. That's the first week of the school holidays. That's when we're having the children's mission, following on the main week.'

'Well surely you don't have to stay for that?'

'I'm running it.'

'You're what?'

'We have all these people coming to lead the mission, and some of them are staying on for the children's week. But I'm organising it. I'm chairing the committee.'

'Good God.' It was the nearest approach Harvey ever got to a prayer.

'So it'll have to be the beginning of August. All right. I'll liaise with the others.'

They discussed dates. I felt a bit like the older brother outside when the father was asking the prodigal son if he wanted the fatted calf well-done, medium or rare. Did I, or did I not, exist?

'You're going to Scotland?' I asked with well-bred reserve.

'In search of the golden eagle,' Delilah answered. 'The same group who went to Lincolnshire.' Where had I heard something about eagles recently? How I would love to see one!

'Would you like to join us?' was the question that I thought was bound to follow. But it never came. I couldn't understand it. I could hardly invite myself. Was Delilah giving me the brush-off? Having landed her fish, was she now abandoning it? Perhaps I could approach her later on her own, but I certainly wasn't going to let Harvey see I wanted an invitation. And come to think of it, if he was one of the party, then perhaps I'd rather not go anyway.

'By the way, Harvey, I'm expecting you to come to the mission.' Delilah moved onto the offensive. She didn't say, 'If I come to Scotland with you, then you must come to the mission with me,' but that seemed to be the implication.

'Not on your life,' returned Harvey cheerfully.

'No. On *your* life! It's your life we're concerned about.'

'Thanks very much. No, full stop.'

'I thought you despised fundamentalists.'

'I do. So what?'

'Do fundamentalists have closed minds or open minds?'

'Closed minds.'

'So are you open-minded or closed-minded?'

'Open-minded, of course.'

' "No" doesn't seem to me the mark of an open mind.'

'I've been into it all, you know that,' said Harvey wearily, lighting a cigarette. 'I've thought it through, and reached my conclusion.'

'You've never given the gospel a chance. You've never really listened to a first-rate speaker putting the case for biblical faith in an adult way.' Delilah was getting out her heavy guns. She was no longer sparring. I was fascinated to see her in action. What was it Sebastian had said? *La belle dame sans merci.*'

'I've listened to you often enough,' he smiled.

'I said a first-rate speaker,' she said with unwonted humility. 'I'm too close to you, anyway. God doesn't usually speak to us through close friends.'

I groaned inwardly. How close was close?

Harvey wriggled. 'We're living in the twentieth century. We've grown up. Man has come of age. It's all outmoded. You're living in the past.' He handed her his cigarette packet.

(Was it really true that talking in platitudes was a sign of an unregenerate man? It sounded plausible.)

'No thanks.' Delilah would not be deflected. 'You're kicking away the ladder, Harvey.'

'The ladder?'

'Not you personally. But this whole generation. We enjoy a superb state of civilisation. We have a welfare state. No one goes hungry. We have a standard of living that would have amazed people a hundred years ago. We have law and order. We have an incredible degree of freedom. We have mobility and choice. We can travel almost anywhere. We have access to education, and culture, and the arts. You needn't talk about the exceptions. Of course I know all about them. Poverty and crime and drugs... But compare our life today with other countries, and other centuries, and you'll see how far we have climbed.'

'All right, I'll admit that.'

'But don't you see, it's the Jewish-Christian tradition that has got us where we are? The laws we take for granted are based on the ten commandments. The values we enjoy come from Christianity. It's Jesus who has taught us the value of the individual, and respect for women, and the importance of children, and care for the weak, and acceptance of foreigners as equals, and the sanctity of life, and every blessed thing.'

Harvey was stunned into silence.

'Rejecting Christ is rejecting the whole basis of our life. It's kicking away the ladder after you have climbed the wall. It's ingratitude. It's rejecting your parents. That's not adulthood. It's adolescence.'

As once before, I saw in Delilah's vehemence something like the wrath of God, the holiness of God, like a flash of light reflected in a window. Perhaps, perhaps, Harvey saw it too. No one moved. The crowded bar with its roar of voices was as unsubstantial as a stage set.

'It's cutting the umbilical cord.'

'Do we have to get physical?' was Harvey's murmured response, which neither deserved nor expected an answer.

Delilah took a plastic carnation from a vase on the

table. She seemed determined to pile metaphor on metaphor.

'*That's* what modern life is.' She held it between finger and thumb, twirling it in front of Harvey's face. 'An imitation of the real thing. Isolated. No roots. Owing nothing to the past. Producing nothing. Dead.'

A long pause followed. Surprisingly, not an embarrassed silence but a pause for thought, relaxed, pregnant and creative. I wondered if anything had given way in Harvey. I prayed.

He smiled a long, slow smile. At least there was something honest about it. It was not his cynical smile. He stubbed out his cigarette, and looked at Delilah.

'I don't believe in God.'

'God believes in you.' Her reply was immediate; thrust and parry; riddle and answer; versicle and response. But it didn't do for Harvey.

'That's patronising.'

'Wouldn't you expect it to be? Patronising means fathering. God is father.'

'It's a nonsensical statement,' he persisted. 'There's no evidence for it. You can't prove it.'

'No, you're right. I can't prove it.' Delilah drained her glass. Had she conceded victory? Had she let Harvey have the last word?

'You can.'

'Me? You must be joking.'

'It's true. I can prove it for me. Jason can prove it for Jason. Only you can prove it for you.'

'How?'

'Think of air,' said Delilah. 'God is very like air. Air is all around us, yet we can't see it. It's also in us.

We can't live without it. We breathe it in, yet we never think about it. We breathe ten times a minute, but we don't have to make a deliberate decision to breathe. "In him we live and move and have our being." Without him we die.'

'It's still all speculation. There's no proof.'

'There are plenty of good ways of proving the existence of air.'

'Such as?'

'Try a parachute jump!' She got up to go.

Harvey looked at his watch. 'Good heavens, is that the time? I must fly.'

'Exactly,' said Delilah. 'Just what I was saying. You must fly. And then jump. I say, Jason, would you be very sweet and pay my bill for me? I really must go. Your office is nearer than mine. I'll pay you back.'

'Of course. Don't bother to pay me back. Let it be on me.' Why hadn't I offered before? I did not offer to pay Harvey's. These estate agents are paid far too much in my opinion.

I waved Delilah goodbye, and watched her slim, tall figure disappearing in the direction of Lower Thames Street. There was no trace of a limp now. Next week we would be playing tennis again. Harvey rushed away.

My work that afternoon was repeatedly interrupted by a vision, a happy daydream, involving Harvey, Delilah and myself. I could not get the picture out of my mind. What I was not sure about was how far this delightful dream had something to do with our personal relationships, and how far it was to be interpreted solely as an indication of Harvey's spiritual need; the need to let God be God;

to put him to the test; to prove his existence by a leap of faith, by falling into his arms. Time would no doubt reveal the right interpretation. Meanwhile, I simply enjoyed the dream, letting my imagination savour every detail.

Harvey, Delilah and I were 20,000 feet up in a plane. Just the three of us; no one else aboard. Delilah was the pilot.

Harvey was wearing a parachute. I sat next to him. He was looking really scared. Delilah shouted above the roar of the engine, 'Now!'

She pulled a lever, and the hatch opened.

Harvey trembled on the brink.

'Go on, now!' shouted Delilah again.

Harvey clung on to a handle.

Then Delilah shouted to me, 'Give him a push, darling.'

I gave Harvey an almighty shove, and down he went. It was a great feeling. I mean, starting him off on his 20,000-foot journey to find God. A privilege.

I watched long enough to see his parachute open out, then I shut the hatch.

Delilah and I flew on into the sunset.

Karen slapped a pile of papers on my desk. Karen is one of our office girls. 'The boss says can you work on these, as he wants them done by first thing in the morning, and would you mind doing overtime?'

Karen filed her nails.

The plane landed with a bump.

12

Space

'Mine!' I called.

'I've got it!' yelled Sebastian at the same time. We muddled, hesitated, then both went for it, clashed racquets and missed.

'Watch it!' said Sebastian. 'You nearly broke my racquet!' A subtle shot from Delilah had gone right down the middle, perfectly placed to have us muddling. She was playing carefully, and her ankle was holding up well. I decided to try some like that myself.

'Forty-thirty,' called Jessica, who was serving. We were on court again, the same four, but this time we were playing girls against boys, and again it was a close-run thing.

Here we were at SPACE, on Saturday evening, and I was surprised there seemed to be so much free time. I had feared it would be a sort of spiritual equivalent to some of the highly pressured and very expensive training weekends my company sometimes laid on. But here, not only the free time but the training sessions too were remarkably relaxed. They almost seemed unstructured. At least there was freedom for flexibility as the weekend went on. Graham called it 'being led by the Spirit'. Anyway within two hours I was glad I had come; after four hours I felt relaxed; and at the end of Friday evening I was really enjoying it, and ready for more. Besides, Brenda had greeted me with the good news that I was to have a room to myself after all.

We finished the set, sweating. The weather had turned hot and humid. There were thundery clouds about. We had time for a dip before supper, and made for the pool. Mandy put down her book, and joined us. She enjoyed bathing. Several people were in the pool already. The sunlight flashed on the blue water. The waves lapped and sucked at the edge. Water splashed over. It was delicious to be in it, up to the neck.

'Fullness' was the word that had stuck in my mind over the past twenty-four hours. Graham had given an opening talk on 'Being filled with the Holy Spirit'. I was interested in the way he took it. He did not talk about a once-for-all catastrophic experience, as I had heard some people do. He talked about a continuous state; a daily experience; gradual growth; degrees of fullness; feelings of fullness and non-feelings; the effect and purpose of fullness—all these things and more came into his talk. And best of all, he talked about emptiness. That was important too.

Now here we were in the pool, and I found myself praying for Mandy, that she would be immersed in blessing, immersed in God's love, as she was in the water. My prayer was a natural movement of tenderness towards someone so frail and vulnerable, yet so

warm and full of life. It was an impulse of the
moment. Nevertheless, I had come to the weekend
with a set purpose to pray for three specific things,
three burdens God had given me; and the first was
Mandy. She headed my prayer list. (My mental
prayer list, that was. I didn't really go along with
those who literally kept lists. It seemed too mechan-
ical.) But I remembered the bit in Matthew, somewhere about the middle, where Jesus teaches about
two or three meeting in his name, and the promise to
two who agree to ask anything in prayer. Although
others had prayed and were praying, I would add my
prayer too. Mandy's total healing was my number
one desire.

Fullness. For her, for me, for everyone, just as the
water lapped our chins. Fullness of life. Life, life,
eternal life!

I suddenly found my mouth and nose more full of
water than I liked. I gasped and struggled up for air.
Sebastian, swimming under water, had torpedoed
me from behind. I might have known it wasn't safe to
be in the same pool with him.

'We'd better get out. Only ten minutes to supper.'

I helped Mandy out, and we dried and dressed.

The food was good and we were all hungry. I
found myself on a table with Delilah and four others
I hardly knew. Jason Enderby, rewrite that last sentence. Yes, Lord. Sorry, Lord. By a clever bit of
scheming I got myself on a table with Delilah and
four others I hardly knew.

It was an unusual sensation to be in a room of a
hundred people all avidly discussing the spiritual
life. Or I imagined they were. The ones on our table
were all going to be fully involved in the mission. As

it turned out, they were on Delilah's committee for the children's week. There was a boy, who seemed absurdly young, who was full of enthusiasm. I recognised him as one of the group who played instruments in church. Malcolm Drake, that was his name.

'I was given a word of knowledge in the meeting this morning,' he was saying. I thought it was rather arrogant of him to claim a word of knowledge, which amounted to a special message from God. (We had been hearing about the gifts of the Spirit, and this was one of them.) Very arrogant. And at his age. But I didn't say so. I merely said, 'How can you be so sure?'

'We can't. Can we, Malcolm?' Delilah cut in quickly, before the youth could answer. 'I'm not sure, and Malcolm isn't sure, but we accept the word in faith, and act on it in faith. Right, Malcolm?'

'I'm quite sure,' he said unabashed. 'The Lord spoke to me.'

Delilah looked at him with amused tolerance.

'Ah. Lucky you. You'll make us all jealous. Nothing personal you realise. "Godly jealousy." 2 Corinthians 11.'

Malcolm persisted on the theme of being sure.

'But you *can* be sure, if it's a word from the Lord,' he said, surprised at her doubting him. 'Surely you are sure, aren't you?'

'Sure,' said Delilah sweetly. (Was she teasing him?) 'But I wouldn't want to be *too* sure, would you?'

'How can you be too sure?'

'Well, let's say, it's good to be absolutely sure and just a little tiny bit unsure.'

'I don't want to be unsure.'

Delilah looked at him.

'Oh dear, Malcolm, I'm sorry for you. Life must be very dull for you. Now my formula for life is 100% faith mixed with x% doubt.'

'Doubt? You, Delilah?' I joined in on Malcolm's side. 'You're a rock-bottom fundamentalist.'

'I'm an open-minded fundamentalist,' she corrected.

'But what do you mean, your formula for life?' said Malcolm. 'Why bring in the doubt?'

'I don't bring it in, my dear boy. It's there. That's the way it is. That's life, as Esther Rantzen would say. And I wouldn't want it any other way.'

She buttered a roll.

'Ever heard of Drake?'

'Drake?'

'Francis Drake. Ancestor of yours, perhaps? He sailed round the world. Now just imagine what that was like. Most people still believed the world was flat. So off he goes, and he's driven by this burning conviction that the world is round, and that he can get right round it. But don't you think there was sometimes a thrill of fear? "What if they're right after all? What if it *is* flat?" I mean, after the first six months you might begin to feel like that, wouldn't you say? And he could never be absolutely sure till he actually sighted Plymouth Hoe again.'

Malcolm chewed his fried plaice in silence.

'What's the world like, Malcolm? Round or flat?' Her cryptic analogy closed that particular conversation. Malcolm, rather chastened, said he'd think about it. I was fascinated to see Delilah on the attack against mindless pietism just as much as against unbelief. But she bathed the wounds she had made.

'Anyway, your word of knowledge,' she went on. 'We really do want to hear about it. I never said it wasn't genuine.'

Malcolm then explained his vision, which was of a spiritual revival among older children, arising from the children's mission. He saw things happening in the secondary schools, and particularly in Brooklands, the local comprehensive where Jessica taught. He looked as if he had not long left school himself.

'That's great, Malcolm,' said Delilah warmly. 'I'll tell Jessica. Maybe she can confirm your word of knowledge. There are one or two others from Brooklands here too. That's something specific to pray for. Let's go for it.'

She was identifying with his boyish enthusiasm now as completely as she had challenged his too-easy assumption of assurance.

We drifted through to the lounge for coffee. Later there was a talk by one of the church leaders ('elders', they called them) on discerning spiritual gifts within the body of Christ, followed by groups in which we were encouraged to talk about the gifts we had, and didn't have, and might have, as individuals, and pray for each other. I felt I had been given the only gift that mattered, the gift of God himself, the reality of Jesus, a new life to live, his Spirit in me—what more could one want? But our group leader told me gently but firmly that gifts were for others, not just for ourselves to enjoy. Which gift did I have that would be a blessing to others? I didn't have a ready answer to this, and the group agreed that this was something to be prayed about during the weekend. I wondered if God was nudging me into getting involved in the mission.

I prayed for Mandy late that night. Perhaps that was my gift. Prayer. Anyway, it seemed all I had to offer for the moment. Again I found my prayer was not asking but trusting. I simply held up Mandy to God, pictured her in the pool, enjoying the water, buoyed up by its solid comfort, at peace. Not me holding her up, but God. Underneath, the everlasting arms.

I was dog-tired, confused with all the teaching and discussion and experiences of the day, yet quietly exhilarated. I was too tired to think logically, yet I went on praying. Almost as if it was God praying, not me. My prayer would have been incoherent, meaningless to anyone listening, yet I knew it was a language God understood, because it was rooted in love and thankfulness. Scraps of poetry flitted across my tongue, lines of hymns, bits from the Prayer Book, Bible verses, phrases that seemed like French (something Sebastian had said?), mindless aspirations (Delilah would not approve), prayer that seemed like a melody line, a lullaby, and ending ingloriously, as lullabies do, in sleep.

I woke next morning with a clear conviction. Mandy was healed. I could not explain it, but I knew it was deeply true. However long she lived, whatever the medical reports, she was safe. Saved. Free. Utterly whole. This was God's answer.

I got on Delilah's table at breakfast. I wanted to tell her. Sebastian was with her. Even with others overhearing, in this sort of atmosphere, it did not seem ridiculous to share what I had experienced. She listened intently. I knew that she believed me, and accepted it. I was thankful.

'Are you sure, Jason?'

There was a momentary pause on the word *sure*. I remembered the conversation with Malcolm.

I reflected. 'I've set sail. I've pushed off from Plymouth Hoe.'

'Splendid. We must go sailing together sometime. Do you sail?'

'I never have. Always ready to learn. Do you?'

'A bit.' So like Delilah, to pass from spiritual to material things, as if there was no distinction. As if sailing and praying were not two things, but one.

'I suppose it's all in *Who's Who*,' I joked. 'Miss Delilah Hewit. Recreations: Tennis, Ornithology, Sailing, Theology…'

'Argument, Bible-bashing, man-baiting,' added Sebastian. We played the *Who's Who* game round the table. Sebastian's recreations, we decided, were Bible-quoting, corny jokes, acronyms and Delilah-teasing. He retaliated.

'Mr Jason Enderby. Recreations: music, bad tennis playing, birdwatching.' I kicked him under the table.

'I was thinking about sailing,' went on Delilah after sanity was restored, 'when Graham was talking about the fullness of the Spirit on Friday night.' She cracked her egg open.

'Tut tut,' said Sebastian. 'Wandering thoughts. Not like you, Del. Fight against them. This will never do. I'll have to tell Graham. "Obey your leaders and submit to their authority" Hebrews 13:17. There's Graham burning his heart out to bring you sound teaching, and you're dreaming about splicing the top mizzen foresail to the starboard gunwale with the main halyard.'

People on the other tables looked round at the explosion of giggles from our table.

'With the marlinspike,' added Sebastian.

'When you've quite finished,' said Delilah, when she could speak, 'it wasn't like that at all. I was listening to every word he said. But it struck me that sailing is the perfect analogy. I mean, this talk about fullness. Of course it's directly scriptural. "Be filled with the Spirit"...' (Sebastian: 'Ephesians 5:18') 'Thank you. But most images of fullness are so totally unhelpful. You know, taking your car to the garage. "Fill her up." "Yes, miss. That'll be £12.40." The Holy Spirit just isn't like that.'

We agreed. I was listening intently. Delilah's theology without tears was always worth listening to, but I was specially interested in this theme. Perhaps my thoughts in the swimming pool were not so helpful after all?

'But picture a yacht. We talk about the sails being filled with wind. That's much nearer the mark. The Spirit is like wind, we all know.' (Sebastian: 'John 3...') 'The sails don't capture the wind. They don't contain it. And you have to keep steering all the time to keep the sail filled. You have to keep a tension on the sheet (rope, to you). It's a matter of delicate balance. It's a living relationship. Surely that's more like the truth? But people talk as if it's like filling a bottle of water. We need to revise our thinking.'

'I am lost,' said Sebastian. 'I mean, lost in admiration. Yes, absolutely. Ready to go about. You're on the right tack, Delilah. I think you should share that with everybody at the next session. It's a word of wisdom.'

As far as I was concerned, every word Delilah

uttered was a word of wisdom. I began to dream of
sailing with Delilah. I abandoned my vision of the
plane, and saw instead Delilah at the helm, Harvey
with a life jacket instead of a parachute, about five
miles out from Cowes; the push; Harvey splashing
and floundering; Delilah and me sailing on into the
sunset...

After breakfast I asked for a word with her alone.
We walked along the terrace. The conference centre
was a large old country house, with modern rooms
added. It was a glorious morning. It was going to be
hot again.

'I hope you don't mind my saying this,' I began.
'It's about Harvey. I'm certainly getting plenty of
challenge from this weekend...' (I was thinking of
the title of SPACE) '...but I wonder if I could put a
sort of challenge to you too. It's just that, when
you're close to someone, you don't always see how
things are going, and maybe someone from outside
can see things more clearly, and...well, I suppose I
shouldn't interfere, but, I mean, this whole weekend,
we're meant to be sharing things, aren't we, and
trying to help each other...'

I was skating round and round. This was being
more difficult than I expected. She was very patient.

'It's just that, I mean, Harvey isn't really respond-
ing, is he? He doesn't seem to be open to the gospel,
does he? He's still basically an atheist, isn't he? And
I wondered if it's right...I mean, it does say, doesn't
it, that we shouldn't be unequally yoked with
unbelievers? Somewhere. I'm sure Sebastian could
tell us where!' I put in, to relieve the tension. I had
been pondering this text for some time. I was glad I
had got it off my chest. At last.

Her smile went right through me, like a laser beam. Fool, why did I have to start this? Her eyebrows went up a little. How I loved that look, though I knew it meant another of her gentle rebukes. Her lips formed themselves into a little round O.

'Yoked?'

She reflected. I waited.

'I never thought of myself as *yoked* to Harvey in any way. St Paul is talking about marriage, isn't he? There's really no question of that!'

I believed her. I realised that she was not yoked to anyone. Perhaps she never would be. She was a mystery. Unique. A virgin queen.

I went on about Harvey. I wanted to show her that I was genuinely concerned about him, and I wasn't motivated by petty jealousy, or anything like that.

'Right. I'm praying for him, as I am sure you are. I really am learning to pray. I came here with certain specific things to pray for.' (I did not mention that there were three things.) 'I've told you about the first—Mandy. Harvey is the second. Do you think prayer is being answered? Do you see any change in him?'

She reflected again.

'No.'

'I agree. That's why I'm praying for him. But I must say, I'm surprised that he doesn't seem to have responded in any way so far. I mean, you've known him for quite a time now, haven't you?'

I secretly wanted to know how long, but she didn't rise. She just said, 'Yes.'

'And you must have got across quite a lot of

teaching during that time. You must have really made him think.'

'You've got a lot to learn, Jason. It isn't teaching that does it. You can't argue someone into the kingdom.'

Good manners prevented me from saying, 'You can have a darn good try!'

'We've got to learn to respect the sovereignty of God,' she went on.

'Yes. Well, I do see that. That's why I'm praying.'

'That's great. Let's keep it up, right? Remember last Sunday's sermon. Yes, no, or wait. This one is obviously wait.'

'Right. I do understand. But I'm still praying specifically that Harvey will come to the mission.'

'So am I. That's good. "If two of you agree about anything you ask for, it will be done for you by my Father." Let's cling to that, shall we?'

'Funny you should mention that. I was thinking of it only yesterday. I read it in Matthew's Gospel.'

'Right. It's a great promise. Chapter 18, I think. We'd better go in. Time for the next session.'

And so our interview ended. I was thankful that in spite of the embarrassment of the subject we ended on a note of agreement, and it was a little comfort to know that she and I were lining up on one side of the fence with Harvey on the other. I needed that reassurance. Scotland still rankled.

We went in. There was some singing. Malcolm and others enjoying themselves up front. There was prayer, relaxed, unhurried. Periods of silence. For the first time in such a gathering I actually prayed myself, out loud. Not for Harvey, or anyone specifically, but a prayer of thanksgiving. It was absolutely spontaneous, and, looking back, absurdly simple and naive. I hoped nobody would think me too idiotic. I just said, 'Lord, thank you, thank you for all this.'

Then there was another talk, continuing the theme of the gifts of the Spirit in each individual, and again we broke into groups. We were a group of nine, none of whom I had known before, yet in two days I had got to know them better than I knew my colleagues at work. We read through 1 Corinthians 12:1–11, and shared our various gifts. When it came to my turn, I rather dreaded that someone was going to say, 'I believe Jason has a gift of prayer!' remembering my contribution that morning. But if anyone thought it, they were too kind to say so. Somebody did say, in all seriousness, 'Have you ever had the experience of speaking in tongues, Jason?'

Ken, our group leader, quickly decided to lighten the mood—tactfully, I thought. Some people do get rather worked up about tongues.

'Of course he has, haven't you Jason? He's an insurance agent. He's got the gift of the gab!'

'Not an *agent* actually,' I corrected him. 'I don't *sell* insurance. No, I haven't got the gift of the gab, and I haven't got the gift of tongues! Just not me. I'm not the type.'

I was fairly certain about that.

'Well, don't be too sure,' said someone else. 'The Holy Spirit sometimes surprises us, you know. I'm certainly not the type, as you call it, but it happened to me.'

'There really isn't any type,' said Ken. 'That's the wonderful thing. Look up verse 11. "He gives them to each man, just as he determines." So if we're really open to the Spirit, God can give any of us the gift, any time.'

'Yes,' said Joan, a woman in her fifties. 'I don't know if this is right, and I've never prayed in tongues in public, but I sometimes find I'm praying in a kind of strange language in bed. Last thing at night. Especially when I'm tired. The Lord seems to take over. It's as if he is singing me to sleep.'

I started. What had she said? I didn't speak any more in that session, but I was thinking hard. Perhaps I would talk to Joan privately later. The session closed.

In the queue going to lunch I encountered Sebastian. There was a mounting volume of noise as everyone gathered. We had to shout to make ourselves heard.

'A good recipe for Babel,' he shouted. 'Take a hundred Pentangles, stir thoroughly, and put together in one room. Babel. Genesis 11. We've been discussing the gift of tongues in our group. Here you have it. The mystery to me is why Paul never mentioned the gift of dumbness. One we really need these days.'

'Pentangles? What do you mean?'

'It's what I call this lot,' he bawled. 'Pentecostal Anglicans. Applies to most of St Paul's people.'

'It doesn't apply to me. You can count me out. Not sure I want to be labelled as a Pentecostal type.'

'No? You surprise me. Just an ordinary angle then. A right angle. No, an obtuse angle. 'Scuse me,' he cut in, before I could think of a retort, 'I must get on that table. Want to talk to Del. I'm joining the DHSS. The Delilah Hewit Suppression Society. Tennis this afternoon? See you at 2.30. If the rain holds off. Bye.' He pushed his way through the crowd.

I was on a table with Mandy for lunch. I looked at her carefully. She did not look any different. But then she had never looked ill anyway. She looked just calmly happy. I supposed, in my darker moments, that this could be what they called a remission. It sometimes happened like that. She might live normally for six months, a year, even two years. Then the blow would fall. And yet, my conviction of the morning was quite genuine. Maybe she was healed. She was certainly at peace with herself, and perhaps that was all that mattered. 'The purpose of life is to live.' Who said that?

'I hope you're getting something out of this, Jason,' she said, as we sat down together. She started serving out the lamb cutlets for the table.

'I really am. It's much better than I thought. I was a bit worried about coming, you know. I didn't quite know what to expect.'

'Naturally. I think most of us felt like that. But everyone seems pretty relaxed now.'

'Absolutely. Relaxed is the word. That's what's so wonderful. I mean, we're all so laid back, and yet things are really happening. It really is God at work, isn't it?'

'I think it is,' she smiled. 'Would you pass the potatoes, please?'

'Sorry. Yes. It's really very refreshing. It gives one a kind of breathing space.'

'That was the intention. Hence the name.'

'Oh. SPACE. Yes. I see. But that's an acronym, isn't it? I mean, St Paul's Away Weekend for whatever it is...'

'Yes, but it's meant to mean *space* as well. That's the whole point. It wasn't one of Sebastian's ideas, you know! Like Mars Bars.'

We both laughed.

'Whose idea was it then?'

'Mine. Well, mine and Delilah's. We worked on it together.'

'Well done you.'

We had coffee together after lunch out on the terrace, and talked and lazed and laughed. She was good to be with. I like Mandy a lot. And it isn't pity.

Again the afternoon was free.

The four of us met for more challenge and enjoyment on the tennis court.

The air was heavy. Good for my sliced backhand. The sun came and went. Black clouds rolled over. People were playing on the other courts too. Others strolled round, or went for walks. Noisy voices came from the swimming pool. Light rain occasionally pattered down, raising the smell of dust. Fifteen all. Thirty–fifteen. Thirty all. Thirty–forty. Deuce. We sweated. The rain came down.

'Let's swim!' cried Delilah. 'It's lovely in the rain.'

In five minutes we were in. The pool was deliciously warm. Delilah and I met.

'I've got a suggestion for you, Jason. Just a thought. A challenge.' She lifted her feet to the end wall of the pool and pushed off, her superb body shooting away towards the other end, as if challenging me to race her. Recreations: Tennis, Ornithology, Sailing, Theology and Swimming. I followed feebly.

'Well, what is it?' I knew she was going to ask me to get involved in the mission.

Wrong.

'You're enjoying your group here?'

'Yes, surprisingly. Yes, I really am. I'm getting a lot from it. I didn't think I would, but I am. Yes.'

'Good.'

She pushed off again towards the other end, I was finding this extraordinary method of conversation rather exhausting, and was getting puffed. After all, we had just played nearly two sets. Was she trying to soften me up for her punchline? I caught up at last, panting.

'What about joining a regular house group?'

She started on another length, leaving me to think out my answer. The rain fell. I was, like Piglet, Entirely Surrounded by Water. Was God trying to tell me something?

I must have been in the pool some time, making my decision, because when I looked round Delilah was out of the water, under cover and drying herself. She came to the edge of the pool and gave me a hand out. I was in rather a dazed condition. But it had been a marvellous swim. I am not a strong swimmer, but I would swim the Hellespont for Delilah. Well, metaphorically speaking.

We got under cover and dried. As soon as I had recovered my breath I faced her.

'Yes. And No.'

I thought this was rather subtle. For once it was fifteen love to me.

'Meaning?'

'Yes, I will join a group. But I think it had better not be yours.'

Nobly, I made that act of renunciation. I knew quite well the danger of being too much under her wing. It was life with Jesus, not life with Delilah, from now on. And she knew it too. That was why, in her wisdom and her kindness, she had not invited me to Scotland.

'A very wise decision. I hoped you'd say that.'

I felt rewarded.

'Thanks for the game,' she grinned.

'Thanks for the swim.'

'Let's go and get some tea.'

We went.

The conference ended with an act of worship which was, for once, all that worship was meant to be. Still with the sensation of rain on my head and shoulders, I felt immersed in God's grace, and I offered to him the third of the concerns with which I had come, my specific matters for prayer. Mandy was the first, Harvey the second. Delilah was the third. The burden, like Christian's, rolled away. The peace which passes all understanding had possession of my heart and mind.

I saw Delilah briefly in the hall, as we were gathering to go out to the car park. A babel of farewells. Everyone was chattering, laughing, embracing. Her face had that bewitching, provocative smile that I had seen so often. She came to say goodbye.

'Refreshed?'

'Absolutely.' I meant it.

'Not too high pressured for you?'

'No. Just right. It really has been—well, space. A breathing space. Just what I needed.'

'Right. We all did. Well, see you sometime. Next Sunday, perhaps, if not before.'

'Yes. Definitely. I'll be there.'

'Don't be too eager.'

She looked straight at me with her mock serious eyes. 'I mean, I know you work so hard, all through the week.'

Witch.

'I think I know how to plan my time,' I smiled. And regretted it. Pompous ass. As if I had a Filofax sticking out of my pocket.

'I'm worried about you, Jason. This decision of yours.'

'Well?'

'This house group idea. Are you sure it's right?'

'I've made my decision,' I answered doggedly.

'For a trial period, of course?'

'Of course. If I don't feel it's right, I can always drop it after a few years!'

'Well, you know best. But if you go to church on Sunday as well, that'll mean twice a week.'

She paused. Angels must have been bustling round her shining presence in that crowded hall. There was silence in heaven for half an hour. I knew then that I would love her for ever, and also that I was free of her for ever.

I almost guessed what would follow.

'You're sure you're not in danger of getting a little too—*avid*?'

There was only one answer to that.

I gave her a smacking kiss.

Married Beyond Recognition

by Sylvia Harney

'Marriage takes a lot of courage. But then so does facing a grizzly bear.'

When boy meets girl, the soft focus and sweet music don't allow for the grim realities of married life. The honeymoon where your new husband reveals a taste for mountain hikes. The first meal: surely fifteen bay leaves are better then one? The unutterable importance of commenting on a clean bathroom after your partner has scrubbed the porcelain half off.

For those contemplating the dread step, *Married Beyond Recognition* is a survival guide. For those of you who aren't, well, celibacy is an option. For those already married, Sylvia Harney's witty insights *might* just help.

SYLVIA HARNEY is a wife, mother and comedienne.

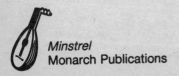

Minstrel
Monarch Publications

The Truth Will Set You Free...

by Jamie Buckingham

No-one escapes the pointed pen of Jamie Buckingham.

Renowned storyteller (even his wife says most of his stories are true) and master satirist, Jamie goes behind the scenes to find targets for his wit and wry observations. Big shots, his friends and family, particularly himself—all are pilloried in this hilarious collection.

Through it all Jamie's keen sense of the ludicrous throws his faith into sharper relief. This book will make you laugh. It may also nudge you a little bit closer to God.

'You ought to try to live with him.'

—Jamie's wife

'If he says another word about my hair transplant, he's fired.'

—One of his publishers

JAMIE BUCKINGHAM is a pastor in Florida and author of many books including *Risky Living, A Way Through the Wilderness* and *Where Eagles Soar.*

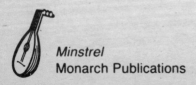

Minstrel
Monarch Publications

The Final Boundary

by Adrian Plass

Life is a rich tapestry of emotions, memories and experience. Adrian Plass is one of the few Christian writers today who reflect that richness, wielding a pen at one moment like an artist's paintbrush, and at the next like a surgeon's knife.

To read these stories is to discover that a parable can 'entertain at the front door while the truth slips in through a side window'...the truth about ourselves, the games we sometimes play and the love we are all searching for.

ADRIAN PLASS, popular writer and broadcaster, has lifted the spirits of hundreds of thousands of readers with his *Sacred Diary* Series. Also in Minstrel paperback from Adrian: *Clearing Away the Rubbish* (Plus cassette).

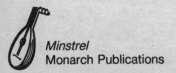

Minstrel
Monarch Publications

Bats In The Belfry

by Murray Watts

'An atheist was lying in the funeral parlour. The mortician put the finishing touches to the body and sighed, "Look at him—all dressed up and nowhere to go."'

This is religious humour with a difference. Not only is it very funny, but also illuminating and sometimes disturbing—a book to cherish. If you need a story to make a point, a joke or open a speech, or simply something to lift your spirits, the solution is at hand!

MURRAY WATTS is an award-winning playwright, whose work has been performed on stage, TV and radio. He is the author of several books including *Laughter in Heaven* and the bestselling *Rolling in the Aisles*.

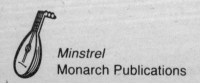

Minstrel
Monarch Publications

Joan 'N' The Whale

by John Duckworth

These fresh and funny parables will make you think about your faith. John Duckworth uses humour, satire and fantasy to offer food for thought on living the Christian life. Cheerful and memorable, his stories hang in the mind. Ideal for the young and the young at heart.

Mad scientist Dr Emil Van Gelical creates 'Christianstein', the greatest specimen of spiritual life the world has ever known, but forgets one crucial ingredient.

After an audit by the Eternal Revenue Service, Mr Carper realises he didn't pay enough thanks.

When a young man calls at a clothes shop to purchase the whole armour of God, he is offered the Sash of Sincerity, the Sports Shirt of Niceness and the Hairspray of Holiness.

'Crackles with inventiveness...very, very funny indeed.' ADRIAN PLASS

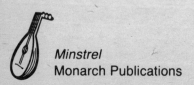

Minstrel
Monarch Publications

Monarch Publications

Monarch Publications was founded to produce books from a Christian perspective which challenge the way people think and feel. Our books are intended to appeal to a very wide constituency, in order to encourage Christian values which currently seem to be in decline.

Monarch Publications has three imprints:

<u>Monarch</u> is concerned with issues, to develop the mind.

<u>MARC</u> is a skills-based list, concentrating on leadership and mission.

<u>Minstrel</u> concentrates on creative writing, to stimulate the imagination.

Monarch Publications is owned by The Servant Trust, a Christian charity run by representatives of the evangelical church in Britain, committed to serve God in publishing and music.

For further information on the Trust, including details of how you may be able to support its work, please write to:

> The Secretary
> The Servant Trust
> 1 St Anne's Road
> Eastbourne
> East Sussex BN21 3UN
> England